PENGUIN BOO

THE THIN M

Dashiell Hammett was born in St Mary's County, Maryland, in 1894. He grew up in Philadelphia and Baltimore. He left school at fourteen, and after that held a variety of jobs, including messenger boy, newsboy, clerk, timekeeper, yardman, machine operator and stevedore, until he finally became an operative for the legendary Pinkerton's Detective Agency. The First World War, however, in which Hammett served as a sergeant, interrupted his sleuthing and shattered his health. When he was finally discharged from the last of several hospitals, he resumed detective work, and subsequently turned to the writing of detective fiction. Now regarded as one of the masters of the genre, Hammett has been a major influence on contemporary fiction. He died in 1961. *The Big Knockover and Other Stories* is also published by Penguin.

THE THIN MAN

DASHIELL HAMMETT

PENGUIN BOOKS

PENGUIN BOOKS

Published by the Penguin Group
Penguin Books Ltd, 27 Wrights Lane, London W8 5TZ, England
Penguin Putnam Inc., 375 Hudson Street, New York, New York 10014, USA
Penguin Books Australia Ltd, Ringwood, Victoria, Australia
Penguin Books Canada Ltd, 10 Alcorn Avenue, Toronto, Ontario, Canada M4V 3B2
Penguin Books (NZ) Ltd, Private Bag 102902, NSMC, Auckland, New Zealand

Penguin Books Ltd, Registered Offices: Harmondsworth, Middlesex, England

First published 1932
Published in Penguin Books 1935
19 20 18

Printed in England by Clays Ltd, St Ives plc
Set in Monotype Baskerville

To
LILLIAN

I

I WAS leaning against the bar in a speakeasy on Fifty-second Street, waiting for Nora to finish her Christmas shopping, when a girl got up from the table where she had been sitting with three other people and came over to me. She was small and blonde, and whether you looked at her face or at her body in powder-blue sports clothes the result was satisfactory. 'Aren't you Nick Charles?' she asked.

I said 'Yes'.

She held out her hand. 'I'm Dorothy Wynant. You don't remember me, but you ought to remember my father, Clyde Wynant. You – '

'Sure,' I said, 'and I remember you now, but you were only a kid of eleven or twelve then, weren't you?'

'Yes, that was eight years ago. Listen: remember those stories you told me? Were they true?'

'Probably not. How is your father?'

She laughed. 'I was going to ask you. Mamma divorced him, you know, and we never hear from him – except when he gets in the newspapers now and then with some of his carryings on. Don't you ever see him?'

My glass was empty. I asked her what she would have to drink, she said Scotch and soda, I ordered two of them and said: 'No, I've been living in San Francisco.'

She said slowly: 'I'd like to see him. Mamma would raise hell if she found it out, but I'd like to see him.'

'Well?'

'He's not where we used to live, on Riverside Drive, and he's not in the phone book or city directory.'

'Try his lawyer,' I suggested.

Her face brightened. 'Who is he?'

'It used to be a fellow named Mac-something-or-other - Macaulay, that's it, Herbert Macaulay. He was in the Singer Building.'

'Lend me a nickel,' she said, and went out to the

telephone. She came back smiling. 'I found him. He's just round the corner on Fifth Avenue.'

'Your father?'

'The lawyer. He says my father's out of town. I'm going round to see him.' She raised her glass to me. 'Family reunions. Look, why don't – '

Asta jumped up and punched me in the belly with her front feet. Nora, at the other end of the leash, said: 'She's had a swell afternoon – knocked over a table of toys at Lord & Taylor's, scared a fat woman silly by licking her leg in Saks's, and has been patted by three policemen.'

I made introductions. 'My wife, Dorothy Wynant. Her father was once a client of mine, when she was only so high. A good guy, but screwy.'

'I was fascinated by him,' Dorothy said, meaning me, 'a real live detective, and used to follow him around making him tell me about his experiences. He told me awful lies, but I believed every word.'

I said: 'You look tired, Nora.'

'I am. Let's sit down.'

Dorothy Wynant said she had to go back to her table. She shook hands with Nora; we must drop in for cocktails, they were living at the Courtland, her mother's name was Jorgensen now. We would be glad to and she must come to see us some time, we were at the Normandie and would be in New York for another week or two. Dorothy patted the dog's head and left us.

We found a table. Nora said: 'She's pretty.'

'If you like them like that.'

She grinned at me. 'You got types?'

'Only you, darling – lanky brunettes with wicked jaws.'

'And how about the red-head you wandered off with at the Quinns' last night?'

'That's silly,' I said. 'She just wanted to show me some French etchings.'

8

II

THE next day Herbert Macaulay telephoned me. 'Hello. I didn't know you were back in town till Dorothy Wynant told me. How about lunch?'

'What time is it?'

'Half past eleven. Did I wake you up?'

'Yes,' I said, 'but that's all right. Suppose you come up here for lunch: I've got a hangover and don't feel like running around much. . . . O.K., say one o'clock.'

I had a drink with Nora, who was going out to have her hair washed, then another after a shower, and was feeling better by the time the telephone rang again.

A female voice asked: 'Is Mr Macaulay there?'

'Not yet.'

'Sorry to trouble you, but would you mind asking him to call his office as soon as he gets there? It's important.'

I promised to do that.

Macaulay arrived about ten minutes later. He was a big, curly-haired, rosy-cheeked, rather good-looking chap of about my age – forty-one – though he looked younger. He was supposed to be a pretty good lawyer. I had worked on several jobs for him when I was living in New York and we had always got along nicely.

Now we shook hands and patted each other's backs, and he asked me how the world was treating me, and I said, 'Fine,' and asked him and he said, 'Fine,' and I told him to call his office.

He came away from the telephone frowning. 'Wynant's back in town,' he said, 'and wants me to meet him.'

I turned around with the drinks I had poured. 'Well, the lunch can – '

'Let him wait,' he said, and took one of the glasses from me.

'Still as screwy as ever?'

'That's no joke,' Macaulay said solemnly. 'You heard

9

they had him in a sanatorium for nearly a year, back in '29?'

'No.'

He nodded. He sat down, put his glass on a table beside his chair, and leaned towards me a little.

'What's Mimi up to, Charles?'

'Mimi? Oh, the wife – the ex-wife. I don't know. Does she have to be up to something?'

'She usually is,' he said dryly, and then very slowly, 'and I thought you'd know.'

So that was it. I said: 'Listen, Mac, I haven't been a detective for six years, since 1927.'

He stared at me.

'On the level,' I assured him. 'A year after I got married, my wife's father died and left her a lumber mill and a narrow-gauge railroad and some other things and I quit the Agency to look after them. Anyway I wouldn't be working for Mimi Wynant, or Jorgensen, or whatever her name is – she never liked me and I never liked her.'

'Oh, I didn't think you – ' Macaulay broke off with a vague gesture and picked up his glass. When he took it away from his mouth, he said: 'I was just wondering. Here Mimi phones me three days ago – Tuesday – trying to find Wynant; then yesterday Dorothy phones, saying you told her to, and comes around, and – I thought you were still sleuthing, so I was wondering what it was all about.'

'Didn't they tell you?'

'Sure – they wanted to see him for old times' sake. That means a lot.'

'You lawyers are a suspicious crew,' I said. 'Maybe they did – that and money. But what's the fuss about? Is he in hiding?'

Macaulay shrugged. 'You know as much about it as I do. I haven't seen him since October.' He drank again. 'How long are you going to be in town?'

'Till after New Year,' I told him and went to the telephone to ask room service for menus.

III

NORA and I went to the opening of *Honeymoon* at the little Theatre that night and then to a party given by some people named Freeman or Fielding or something. I felt pretty low when she called me the next morning. She gave me a newspaper and a cup of coffee and said: 'Read that.'

I patiently read a paragraph or two, then put the paper down and took a sip of coffee. 'Fun's fun,' I said, 'but right now I'd swap you all the interviews with Mayor-elect O'Brien ever printed – and throw in the Indian picture – for a slug of whis – '

'Not that, stupid.' She put a finger on the paper 'That.'

INVENTOR'S SECRETARY
MURDERED IN APARTMENT

JULIA WOLF'S BULLET-RIDDLED BODY FOUND; POLICE
SEEK HER EMPLOYER, CLYDE WYNANT

'The bullet-riddled body of Julia Wolf, thirty-two-year-old confidential secretary to Clyde Miller Wynant, well-known inventor, was discovered late yesterday afternoon in the dead woman's apartment at 411 East Fifty-fourth St by Mrs Christian Jorgensen, divorced wife of the inventor, who had gone there in an attempt to learn her former husband's present address.

'Mrs Jorgensen, who returned Monday after a six-year stay in Europe, told police that she heard feeble groans when she rang the murdered woman's door-bell, whereupon she notified an elevator boy, Mervin Holly, who called Walter Meany, apartment-house superintendent. Miss Wolf was lying on the bedroom floor with four ·32-calibre bullet wounds in her chest when they entered the apartment, and died without having recovered consciousness before police and medical aid arrived.

'Herbert Macaulay, Wynant's attorney, told the police

that he had not seen the inventor since October. He stated that Wynant called him on the telephone yesterday and made an appointment, but failed to keep it; and disclaimed any knowledge of his client's whereabouts. Miss Wolf, Macaulay stated, had been in the inventor's employ for the past eight years. The attorney said he knew nothing about the dead woman's family or private affairs and could throw no light on her murder.

'The bullet-wounds could not have been self-inflicted, according to. . . .'

The rest of it was the usual police department hand-out.

'Do you suppose he killed her?' Nora asked when I put the paper down again.

'Wynant? I wouldn't be surprised. He's batty as hell.'

'Did you know her?'

'Yes. How about a drop of something to cut the phlegm?'

'What was she like?'

'Not bad,' I said. 'She wasn't bad-looking and she had a lot of sense and a lot of nerve – and it took both to live with that guy.'

'She lived with him?'

'Yes. I want a drink, please. That is, it was like that when I knew them.'

'Why don't you have some breakfast first? Was she in love with him or was it just business?'

'I don't know. It's too early for breakfast.'

When Nora opened the door to go out, the dog came in and put her front feet on the bed, her face in my face. I rubbed her head and tried to remember something Wynant had once said to me, something about women and dogs. It was not the woman–spaniel–walnut-tree line. I could not remember what it was, but there seemed to be some point in trying to remember.

Nora returned with two drinks and another question: 'What's he like?'

'Tall – over six feet – and one of the thinnest men I've ever seen. He must be about fifty now, and his hair was

12

almost white when I knew him. Usually needs a haircut, ragged brindle moustache, bites his fingernails.' I pushed the dog away to reach for my drink.

'Sounds lovely. What were you doing with him?'

'A fellow who'd worked for him accused him of stealing some kind of idea or invention from him. Rosewater was his name. He tried to shake Wynant down by threatening to shoot him, bomb his house, kidnap his children, cut his wife's throat – I don't know what all – if he didn't come across. We never caught him – must've scared him off. Anyway, the threats stopped and nothing happened.'

Nora stopped drinking to ask: 'Did Wynant really steal it?'

'Tch, tch, tch,' I said. 'This is Christmas Eve: try to think good of your fellow-man.'

IV

THAT afternoon I took Asta for a walk, explained to two people that she was a Schnauzer and not a cross between a Scottie and an Irish terrier, stopped at Jim's for a couple of drinks, ran into Larry Crowley, and brought him back to the Normandie with me. Nora was pouring cocktails for the Quinns, Margot Innes, a man whose name I did not catch, and Dorothy Wynant.

Dorothy said she wanted to talk to me, so we carried our cocktails into the bedroom.

She came to the point right away. 'Do you think my father killed her, Nick?'

'No,' I said. 'Why should I?'

'Well, the police have – Listen, she was his mistress, wasn't she?'

I nodded. 'When I knew them.'

She stared at her glass while saying: 'He's my father. I never liked him. I never liked Mamma.' She looked up at me. 'I don't like Gilbert.' Gilbert was her brother.

'Don't let that worry you. Lots of people don't like their relatives.'

'Do you like them?'

'My relatives?'

'Mine.' She scowled at me. 'And stop talking to me as if I was still twelve.'

'It's not that,' I explained. 'I'm getting tight.'

'Well, do you?'

I shook my head. 'You were all right, just a spoiled kid. I could get along without the rest of them.'

'What's the matter with us?' she asked, not argumentatively, but as if she really wanted to know.

'Different things. Your – '

Harrison Quinn opened the door and said: 'Come on over and play some ping-pong, Nick.'

'In a little while.'

'Bring beautiful along.' He leered at Dorothy and went away.

She said: 'I don't suppose you know Jorgensen.'

'I know a Nels Jorgensen.'

'Some people have all the luck. This one's named Christian. He's a honey. That's Mamma – divorces a lunatic and marries a gigolo.' Her eyes became wet. She caught her breath in a sob and asked: 'What am I going to do, Nick?' Her voice was a frightened child's.

I put an arm around her and made what I hoped were comforting sounds. She cried on my lapel. The telephone beside the bed began to ring. In the next room *Rise and Shine* was coming through the radio. My glass was empty. I said: 'Walk out on them.'

She sobbed again. 'You can't walk out on yourself.'

'Maybe I don't know what you're talking about.'

'Please don't tease me,' she said humbly.

Nora, coming in to answer the telephone, looked questioningly at me. I made a face at her over the girl's head.

When Nora said 'Hello' into the telephone, the girl

14

stepped quickly back away from me and blushed. 'I – I'm sorry,' she stammered, 'I didn't – '

Nora smiled sympathetically at her. I said: 'Don't be a dope.' The girl found her handkerchief and dabbed at her eyes with it.

Nora spoke into the telephone: 'Yes. . . . I'll see if he's in. Who's calling, please?' She put a hand over the mouthpiece and adressed me: 'It's a man named Norman. Do you want to talk to him?'

I said I didn't know and took the telephone. 'Hello.'

A somewhat harsh voice said: 'Mr Charles? . . . Mr Charles, I understand that you were formerly connected with the Trans-American Detective Agency.'

'Who is this?' I asked.

'My name is Albert Norman, Mr Charles, which probably means nothing to you, but I would like to lay a proposition before you. I am sure you will – '

'What kind of proposition?'

'I can't discuss it over the phone, Mr Charles, but if you will give me half an hour of your time, I can promise – '

'Sorry,' I said. 'I'm pretty busy and – '

'But, Mr Charles, this is – ' Then there was a loud noise: it could have been a shot or something falling or anything else that would make a loud noise. I said: 'Hello,' a couple of times, got no answer, and hung up.

Nora had Dorothy over in front of a looking-glass soothing her with powder and rouge. I said: 'A guy selling insurance,' and went into the living-room for a drink.

Some more people had come in. I spoke to them. Harrison Quinn left the sofa where he had been sitting with Margot Innes and said: 'Now ping-pong.' Asta jumped up and punched me in the belly with her front feet. I shut off the radio and poured myself a cocktail. The man whose name I had not caught was saying: 'Comes the revolution and we'll all be lined up against the wall – first thing.' He seemed to think it was a good idea.

Quinn came over to refill his glass. He looked towards

the bedroom door. 'Where'd you find the little blonde?'

'Used to bounce it on my knee.'

'Which knee?' he asked. 'Could I touch it?'

Nora and Dorothy came out of the bedroom. I saw an afternoon paper on the radio and picked it up. Headlines said:

JULIA WOLF ONCE RACKETEER'S GIRL
ARTHUR NUNHEIM IDENTIFIES BODY
WYNANT STILL MISSING

Nora, at my elbow, spoke in a low voice: 'I asked her to have dinner with us. Be nice to the child' – Nora was twenty-six – 'she's all upset.'

'Whatever you say.' I turned around. Dorothy, across the room, was laughing at something Quinn was telling her. 'But if you get mixed up in people's troubles, don't expect me to kiss you where you're hurt.'

'I won't. You're a sweet old fool. Don't read that here now.' She took the newspaper away from me and stuck it out of sight behind the radio.

V

NORA could not sleep that night. She read Chaliapin's memoirs until I began to doze and then woke me up by saying: 'Are you asleep?'

I said I was.

She lit a cigarette for me, one for herself. 'Don't you ever think you'd like to go back to detecting once in a while just for the fun of it? You know, when something special comes up, like the Lindb – '

'Darling,' I said, ' my guess is that Wynant killed her, and the police'll catch him without my help. Anyway, it's nothing in my life.'

'I didn't mean just that, but – '

'But besides I haven't the time: I'm too busy trying to

see that you don't lose any of the money I married you for.' I kissed her. 'Don't you think maybe a drink would help you to sleep?'

'No thanks.'

'Maybe it would if I took one.' When I brought my Scotch and soda back to bed, she was frowning into space.

I said: 'She's cute, but she's cuckoo. She wouldn't be his daughter if she wasn't. You can't tell how much of what she says is what she thinks and you can't tell how much of what she thinks ever really happened. I like her, but I think you're letting – '

'I'm not sure I like her,' Nora said thoughtfully, 'she's probably a little brat, but if a quarter of what she told us is true, she's in a tough spot.'

'There's nothing I can do to help her.'

'She thinks you can.'

'And so do you, which shows that no matter what you think, you can always get somebody else to go along with you.'

Nora sighed. 'I wish you were sober enough to talk to.' She leaned over to take a sip of my drink. 'I'll give you your Christmas present now if you'll give me mine.'

I shook my head. 'At breakfast.'

'But it's Christmas now.'

'Breakfast.'

'Whatever you're giving me,' she said, 'I hope I don't like it.'

'You'll have to keep them anyway, because the man at the Aquarium said he positively wouldn't take them back. He said they'd already bitten the tails off the – '

'It wouldn't hurt you any to find out if you can help her, would it? She's got so much confidence in you, Nicky.'

'Everybody trusts Greeks.'

'Please.'

'You just want to poke your nose into things that – '

'I meant to ask you: did his wife know the Wolf girl was his mistress?'

17

'I don't know. She didn't like her.'

'What's the wife like?'

'I don't know – a woman.'

'Good-looking?'

'Used to be very.'

'She old?'

'Forty, forty-two. Cut it out, Nora. You don't want any part of it. Let the Charleses stick to the Charleses' troubles and the Wynants stick to the Wynants'.'

She pouted. 'Maybe that drink would help me.'

I got out of bed and mixed a drink. As I brought it into the bedroom, the telephone began to ring. I looked at my watch on the table. It was nearly five o'clock.

Nora was talking into the telephone: 'Hello. . . . Yes, speaking.' She looked sidewise at me. I shook my head no. 'Yes. . . . Why, certainly. . . . Yes, certainly.' She put the telephone down and grinned at me.

'You're wonderful,' I said. 'Now what?'

'Dorothy's coming up. I think she's tight.'

'That's great.' I picked up my bathrobe: 'I was afraid I was going to have to go to sleep.'

She was bending over looking for her slippers. 'Don't be such an old fuff. You can sleep all day.' She found her slippers and stood up in them. 'Is she really as afraid of her mother as she says?'

'If she's got any sense. Mimi's poison.'

Nora screwed up her dark eyes at me and asked slowly: 'What are you holding out on me?'

'Oh dear,' I said, 'I was hoping I wouldn't have to tell you. Dorothy is really my daughter. I didn't know what I was doing, Nora. It was spring in Venice and I was so young and there was a moon over the – '

'Be funny. Don't you want something to eat?'

'If you do. What do you want?'

'Raw chopped beef sandwich with a lot of onion and some coffee.'

Dorothy arrived while I was telephoning an all-night

delicatessen. When I went into the living-room, she stood up with some difficulty and said: 'I'm awfully sorry, Nick, to keep bothering you and Nora like this, but I can't go home this way tonight. I can't. I'm afraid to. I don't know what'd happen to me, what I'd do. Please don't make me.' She was very drunk. Asta sniffed at her ankles.

I said: 'Sh-h-h. You're all right here. Sit down. There'll be some coffee in a little while. Where'd you get the snoutful?'

She sat down and shook her head stupidly. 'I don't know. I've been everywhere since I left you. I've been everywhere except home because I can't go home this way. Look what I got.' She stood up again and took a battered automatic pistol out of her coat pocket. 'Look at that.' She waved it at me while Asta, wagging her tail, jumped happily at it.

Nora made a noise with her breathing. The back of my neck was cold. I pushed the dog aside and took the pistol away from Dorothy. 'What kind of clowning is this? Sit down.' I dropped the pistol into the bathrobe pocket and pushed Dorothy down in her chair.

'Don't be mad at me, Nick,' she whined. 'You can keep it. I don't want to make a nuisance of myself.'

'Where'd you get it?' I asked.

'In a speakeasy on Tenth Avenue. I gave a man my bracelet – the one with the emeralds and diamonds – for it.'

'And then won it back from him in a crap game,' I said. 'You've still got it on.'

She stared at her bracelet. 'I thought I did.'

I looked at Nora and shook my head. Nora said: 'Aw, don't bully her, Nick. She's – '

'He's not bullying me, Nora, he's really not.' Dorothy said quickly. 'He's – he's the only person I got in the world to turn to.'

I remembered Nora had not touched her Scotch and soda, so I went into the bedroom and drank it. When I came back, Nora was sitting on the arm of Dorothy's chair with an arm around the girl. Dorothy was sniffling; Nora

was saying: 'But Nick's not mad, dear. He likes you.'
She looked up at me. 'You're not mad, are you, Nicky?'

'No, I'm just hurt.' I sat on the sofa. 'Where'd you get the gun, Dorothy?'

'From a man – I told you.'

'What man?'

'I told you – a man in a speakeasy.'

'And you gave him a bracelet for it.'

'I thought I did, but – look – I've still got my bracelet.'

'I noticed that.'

Nora patted the girl's shoulder. 'Of course you've still got your bracelet.'

I said: 'When the boy comes with that coffee and stuff, I'm going to bribe him to stick around. I'm not going to stay alone with a couple of – '

Nora scowled at me, told the girl: 'Don't mind him. He's been like that all night.'

The girl said: 'He thinks I'm a silly little drunken fool.' Nora patted her shoulder some more.

I asked: 'But what'd you want a gun for?'

Dorothy sat up straight and stared at me with wide drunken eyes. 'Him,' she whispered excitedly, 'if he bothered me. I was afraid because I was drunk. That's what it was. And then I was afraid of that, too, so I came here.'

'You mean your father?' Nora asked, trying to keep excitement out of her voice.

The girl shook her head. 'Clyde Wynant's my father. My stepfather.' She leaned against Nora's breast.

Nora said: 'Oh,' in a tone of very complete understanding. Then she said: 'You poor child,' and looked significantly at me.

I said: 'Let's all have a drink.'

'Not me.' Nora was scowling at me again. 'And I don't think Dorothy wants one.'

'Yes, she does. It'll help her sleep.' I poured her a terrific dose of Scotch and saw that she drank it. It worked nicely:

she was sound asleep by the time our coffee and sandwiches came.

Nora said: 'Now you're satisfied.'

'Now I'm satisfied. Shall we tuck her in before we eat?'

I carried her into the bedroom and helped Nora undress her. She had a beautiful little body.

We went back to our food. I took the pistol out of my pocket and examined it. It had been kicked around a lot. There were two cartridges in it, one in the chamber, one in the magazine.

'What are you going to do with it?' Nora asked.

'Nothing till I find out if it's the one Julia Wolf was killed with. It's a ·32.'

'But she said – '

'She got it in a speakeasy – from a man – for a bracelet. I heard her.'

Nora leaned over her sandwich at me. Her eyes were very shiny and almost black. 'Do you suppose she got it from her stepfather?'

'I do,' I said, but I said it too earnestly.

Nora said: 'You're a Greek louse. But maybe she did; you don't know. And you don't believe her story.'

'Listen, darling, tomorrow I'll buy you a whole lot of detective stories, but don't worry your pretty little head over mysteries tonight. All she was trying to tell you was that she was afraid Jorgensen was waiting to try to make her when she got home and she was afraid she was drunk enough to give in!'

'But her mother!'

'This family's a family. You can – '

Dorothy Wynant, standing unsteadily in the doorway in a nightgown much too long for her, blinked at the light and said: 'Please, can I come in for a little while? I'm afraid in there alone.'

'Sure.'

She came over and curled up beside me on the sofa while Nora went to get something to put around her.

VI

THE three of us were at breakfast early that afternoon when the Jorgensens arrived. Nora answered the telephone and came away from it trying to pretend she was not tickled. 'It's your mother,' she told Dorothy. 'She's downstairs. I told her to come up.'

Dorothy said: 'Damn it. I wish I hadn't phoned her.'

I said: 'We might just as well be living in the lobby.'

Nora said: 'He doesn't mean that.' She patted Dorothy's shoulder.

The door-bell rang. I went to the door.

Eight years had done no damage to Mimi's looks. She was a little riper, showier, that was all. She was larger than her daughter, and her blondness was more vivid. She laughed and held her hands out to me. 'Merry Christmas. It's awfully good to see you after all these years. This is my husband. Mr Charles, Chris.'

I said: 'I'm glad to see you, Mimi,' and shook hands with Jorgensen. He was probably five years younger than his wife, a tall, thin, erect, dark man, carefully dressed and sleek, with smooth hair and a waxed moustache.

He bowed from the waist. 'How do you do, Mr Charles?' His accent was heavy, Teutonic, his hand was lean and muscular.

We went inside.

Mimi, when the introductions were over, apologized to Nora for popping in on us. 'But I did want to see your husband again, and then I know the only way to get this brat of mine anywhere on time is to carry her off bodily.' She turned her smile on Dorothy. 'Better get dressed, honey.'

Honey grumbled through a mouthful of toast that she didn't see why she had to waste an afternoon at Aunt Alice's even if it was Christmas. 'I bet Gilbert's not going.'

Mimi said Asta was a lovely dog and asked me if I

had *any* idea where that ex-husband of hers might be.

'No.'

She went on playing with the dog. 'He's crazy, absolutely crazy, to disappear at a time like this. No wonder the police at first thought he had something to do with it.'

'What do they think now?' I asked.

She looked up at me. 'Haven't you seen the papers?'

'No.'

'It's a man named Morelli – a gangster. He killed her. He was her lover.'

'They caught him?'

'Not yet, but he did it. I wish I could find Clyde. Macaulay won't help me at all. He says he doesn't know where he is, but that's ridiculous. He has powers of attorney from him and everything and I know very well he's in touch with Clyde. Do you think Macaulay's trustworthy?'

'He's Wynant's lawyer,' I said. 'There's no reason why you should trust him.'

'Just what I thought.' She moved over a little on the sofa. 'Sit down. I've got millions of things to ask you.'

'How about a drink first?'

'Anything but egg-nog,' she said. 'It makes me bilious.'

When I came out of the pantry, Nora and Jorgensen were trying their French on each other, Dorothy was still pretending to eat, and Mimi was playing with the dog again. I distributed the drinks and sat down beside Mimi.

She said: 'Your wife's lovely.'

'I like her.'

'Tell me the truth, Nick: do you think Clyde's really crazy? I mean crazy enough that something ought to be done about it.'

'How do I know?'

'I'm worried about the children,' she said. 'I've no claim on him any more – the settlement he made when I divorced him took care of all that – but the children have. We're absolutely penniless now and I'm worried about them. If he is crazy he's just as likely as not to throw away everything

23

and leave them without a cent. What do you think I ought to do?'

'Thinking about putting him in the booby-hatch?'

'No – o,' she said slowly, 'but I would like to talk to him.' She put a hand on my arm. 'You could find him.'

I shook my head.

'Won't you help me, Nick? We used to be friends.' Her big blue eyes were soft and appealing.

Dorothy, at the table, was watching us suspiciously.

'For Christ's sake Mimi,' I said, 'there's a thousand detectives in New York. Hire one of them. I'm not working at it any more.'

'I know, but – Was Dorry very drunk last night?'

'Maybe I was. She seemed all right to me.'

'Don't you think she's got to be a pretty little thing?'

'I always thought she was.'

She thought that over for a moment, then said: 'She's only a child, Nick.'

'What's that got to do with what?' I asked.

She smiled. 'How about getting some clothes on, Dorry?'

Dorothy sulkily repeated that she didn't see why she had to waste an afternoon at Aunt Alice's.

Jorgensen turned to address his wife: 'Mrs Charles has the great kindness to suggest that we do not – '

'Yes,' Nora said, 'why don't you stay a while? There'll be some people coming in. It won't be very exciting, but – ' She waved her glass a little to finish the sentence.

'I'd love to,' Mimi replied slowly, 'but I'm afraid Alice – '

'Make our apologies to her by telephone,' Jorgensen suggested.

'I'll do it,' Dorothy said.

Mimi nodded. 'Be nice to her.'

Dorothy went into the bedroom. Everybody seemed much brighter. Nora caught my eye and winked merrily and I had to take it and like it because Mimi was looking at me then.

Mimi asked me: 'You really didn't want us to stay, did you?'

'Of course.'

'Chances are you're lying. Weren't you sort of fond of poor Julia?'

'"Poor Julia" sounds swell from you. I liked her all right.'

Mimi put her hand on my arm again. 'She broke up my life with Clyde. Naturally I hated her – then – but that's a long time ago. I had no feeling against her when I went to see her Friday. And, Nick, I saw her die. She didn't deserve to die. It was horrible. No matter what I'd felt, there'd be nothing left but pity now. I meant "poor Julia" when I said it.'

'I don't know what you're up to,' I said. 'I don't know what any of you are up to.'

'Any of us,' she repeated. 'Has Dorry been – '

Dorothy came in from the bedroom. 'I squared it.' She kissed her mother on the mouth and sat down beside her.

Mimi, looking in her compact-mirror to see her mouth had not been smeared, asked: 'She wasn't peevish about it?'

'No, I squared it. What do you have to do to get a drink?'

I said: 'You have to walk over to that table where the ice and bottles are and pour it.'

Mimi said: 'You drink too much.'

'I don't drink as much as Nick.' She went over to the table.

Mimi shook her head. 'These children! I mean you were pretty fond of Julia Wolf, weren't you?'

Dorothy called: 'You want one, Nick?'

'Thanks,' I said; then to Mimi, 'I liked her well enough.'

'You're the damnedest evasive man,' she complained. 'Did you like her as much as you used to like me, for instance?'

'You mean those couple of afternoons we killed?'

Her laugh was genuine. 'That's certainly an answer.'

She turned to Dorothy, carrying glasses towards us.

25

'You'll have to get a robe that shade of blue, darling. It's very becoming to you.'

I took one of the glasses from Dorothy and said I thought I had better get dressed.

VII

WHEN I came out of the bathroom, Nora and Dorothy were in the bedroom, Nora combing her hair, Dorothy sitting on the side of the bed dangling a stocking.

Nora made a kiss at me in the dressing-table mirror. She looked very happy.

'You like Nick, don't you, Nora?' Dorothy asked.

'He's an old Greek fool, but I'm used to him.'

'Charles isn't a Greek name.'

'It's Charalambides,' I explained. 'When the old man came over, the mug that put him through Ellis Island said Charalambides was too long – too much trouble to write – and whittled it down to Charles. It was all right with the old man; they could have called him X so they let him in.'

Dorothy stared at me. 'I never know when you're lying.' She started to put on the stocking, stopped. 'What's Mamma trying to do to you?'

'Nothing. Pump me. She'd like to know what you did and said last night.'

'I thought so. What'd you tell her?'

'What could I tell her? You didn't do or say anything.'

She wrinkled her forehead over that, but when she spoke again it was about something else: 'I never knew there was anything between you and Mamma. Of course I was only a kid then and wouldn't have known what it was all about even if I'd noticed anything, but I didn't even know you called each other by your first names.'

Nora turned from the mirror laughing. 'Now we're getting somewhere.' She waved the comb at Dorothy. 'Go on, dear.'

Dorothy said earnestly: 'Well, I didn't know.'

I was taking laundry pins out of a shirt. 'What do you know now?' I asked.

'Nothing,' she said slowly, and her face began to grow pink, 'but I can guess.' She bent over her stocking.

'Can and do,' I growled. 'You're a dope, but don't look so embarrassed. You can't help it if you've got a dirty mind.'

She raised her head and laughed, but when she asked: 'Do you think I take after Mamma much?' she was serious.

'I wouldn't be surprised.'

'But do you?'

'You want me to say no. No.'

'That's what I have to live with,' Nora said cheerfully. 'You can't do anything with him.'

I finished dressing first and went out to the living-room. Mimi was sitting on Jorgensen's knees. She stood up and asked: 'What'd you get for Christmas?'

'Nora gave me a watch.' I showed it to her.

She said it was lovely, and it was. 'What'd you give her?'

'Necklace.'

Jorgensen said: 'May I?' and rose to mix himself a drink.

The door-bell rang. I let the Quinns and Margot Innes in, introducing them to the Jorgensens. Presently Nora and Dorothy finished dressing and came out of the bedroom and Quinn attached himself to Dorothy. Larry Crowley arrived, with a girl named Denis, and a few minutes later the Edges. I won thirty-two dollars – on the cuff – from Margot at backgammon. The Denis girl had to go into the bedroom and lie down a while. Alice Quinn, with Margot's help, tore her husband away from Dorothy at a little after six and carried him off to keep a date they had. The Edges left. Mimi put on her coat, got her husband and daughter into their coats.

'It's awful short notice,' she said, 'but can't you come to dinner tomorrow night?'

Nora said: 'Certainly.'

We shook hands and made polite speeches all around and they went away.

Nora shut the door after them and leaned her back against it. 'God, he's a handsome guy,' she said.

VIII

So far I had known just where I stood on the Wolf-Wynant-Jorgensen troubles and what I was doing – the answers were, respectively, nowhere and nothing – but when we stopped at Reuben's for coffee on our way home at four the next morning, Nora opened a newspaper and found a line in one of the gossip columns: 'Nick Charles, former Trans-American Detective Agency ace, in from Coast to sift the Julia Wolf murder mystery'; and when I opened my eyes and sat up in bed some six hours later Nora was shaking me and a man with a gun in his hand was standing in the bedroom doorway.

He was a plump, dark, youngish man of medium height, broad through the jaws, narrow between the eyes. He wore a black bowler hat, a black overcoat that fitted him very snugly, a dark suit, and black shoes, all looking as if he had bought them within the past fifteen minutes. The gun, a blunt black ·38-calibre automatic, lay comfortably in his hand, not pointing at anything.

Nora was saying: 'He made me let him in, Nick. He said he had to – '

'I got to talk to you,' the man with the gun said. 'That's all, but I got to do that.' His voice was low and rasping.

I had blinked myself awake by then. I looked at Nora. She was excited, but apparently not frightened: she might have been watching a horse she had a bet on coming down the stretch with a nose lead.

I said: 'All right, talk, but do you mind putting the gun away?'

He smiled with his lower lip. 'You don't have to tell me you're tough. I heard about you.' He put the pistol in his overcoat pocket. 'I'm Shep Morelli.'

'I never heard about you,' I said.

He took a step into the room and began to shake his head from side to side. 'I didn't knock Julia off.'

'Maybe you didn't, but you're bringing the news to the wrong place. I got nothing to do with it.'

'I haven't seen her in three months,' he said. 'We were washed up.'

'Tell the police.'

'I wouldn't have any reason to hurt her: she was always on the up and up with me.'

'That's all swell,' I said, 'only you're peddling your fish in the wrong market.'

'Listen.' He took another step towards the bed. 'Studsy Burke tells me you used to be O.K. That's why I'm here. Do the – '

'How is Studsy?' I asked. 'I haven't seen him since the time he went up the river in '23 or '24.'

'He's all right. He'd like to see you. He's got a joint on West Forty-ninth, the Pigiron Club. But listen, what's the law doing to me? Do they think I did it? Or is it just something else to pin on me?'

I shook my head. 'I'd tell you if I knew. Don't let newspapers fool you: I'm not in this. Ask the police.'

'That'd be very smart.' He smiled with his lower lip again. 'That'd be the smartest thing I ever did. Me that a police captain's been in a hospital three weeks on account we had an argument. The boys would like me to come in and ask 'em questions. They'd like it right down to the end of their black-jacks.' He turned a hand over, palm up. 'I come to you on the level. Studsy says you're on the level. Be on the level.'

'I'm being on the level,' I assured him. 'If I knew anything I'd – '

Knuckles drummed on the corridor door, three times,

sharply. Morelli's gun was in his hand before the noise stopped. His eyes seemed to move in all directions at once. His voice was a metallic snarl deep in his chest: 'Well?'

'I don't know.' I sat up a little higher in bed and nodded at the gun in his hand. 'That makes it your party.' The gun pointed very accurately at my chest. I could hear the blood in my ears, and my lips felt swollen. I said: 'There's no fire-escape.' I put my left hand out towards Nora, who was sitting on the far side of the bed.

The knuckles hit the door again, and a deep voice called: 'Open up. Police.'

Morelli's lower lip crawled up to lap the upper, and the whites of his eyes began to show under the irises. 'You rat,' he said slowly, almost as if he were sorry for me. He moved his feet the least bit, flattening them against the floor.

A key touched the outer lock.

I hit Nora with my left hand, knocking her down across the room. The pillow I chucked with my right hand at Morelli's gun seemed to have no weight; it drifted slow as a piece of tissue paper. No noise in the world, before or after, was ever so loud as Morelli's gun going off. Something pushed my left side as I sprawled across the floor. I caught one of his ankles and rolled over with it, bringing him down on me, and he clubbed my back with the gun until I got a hand free and began to hit him as low in the body as I could.

Men came in and dragged us apart.

It took us five minutes to bring Nora to.

She sat up holding her cheek and looked around the room until she saw Morelli, nippers on one wrist, standing between two detectives. Morelli's face was a mess; the coppers had worked him over a little just for the fun of it. Nora glared at me: 'You damned fool,' she said, 'you didn't have to knock me cold. I knew you'd take him, but I wanted to see it.'

One of the coppers laughed. 'God,' he said admiringly, 'there's a woman with grit.'

She smiled at him and stood up. When she looked at me she stopped smiling. 'Nick, you're – '

I said I didn't think it was much and opened what was left of my pyjama-coat. Morelli's bullet had scooped out a gutter perhaps four inches long under my left nipple. A lot of blood was running out of it, but it was not very deep.

Morelli said: 'Tough luck. A couple of inches over would make a lot of difference the right way.'

The copper who had admired Nora – he was a big, sandy man of forty-eight or fifty in a grey suit that did not fit him very well – slapped Morelli's mouth.

Keyser, the Normandie's manager, said he would get a doctor and went to the telephone. Nora ran to the bathroom for towels.

I put a towel over the wound and lay down on the bed. 'I'm all right. Don't let's fuss over it till the doctor comes. How'd you people happen to pop in?'

The copper who had slapped Morelli said: 'We happen to hear this is getting to be kind of a meeting-place for Wynant's family and his lawyer and everybody, so we think we'll kind of keep an eye on it in case he happens to show up, and this morning when Mac here, who was the eye we were kind of keeping on it at the time, sees this bird duck in, he gives us a ring and we get hold of Mr Keyser and come on up, and pretty lucky for you.'

'Yes, pretty lucky for me, or maybe I wouldn't've got shot.'

He eyed me suspiciously. His eyes were pale grey and watery. 'This bird a friend of yours?'

'I never saw him before.'

'What'd he want of you?'

'Wanted to tell me he didn't kill the Wolf girl.'

'What's that to you?'

'Nothing.'

'What'd he think it was to you?'

'Ask him. I don't know.'

'I'm asking you.'

31

'Keep on asking.'

'I'll ask you another one: you're going to swear to the complaint on him shooting you?'

'That's another one I can't answer right now. Maybe it was an accident.'

'Oke. There's plenty of time. I guess we got to ask you a lot more things than we'd figured on.' He turned to one of his companions: there were four of them. 'We'll frisk this joint.'

'Not without a warrant,' I told him.

'So you say. Come on, Andy.' They began to search the place.

The doctor – a colourless wisp of a man with the snuffles – came in, clucked and sniffed over my side, got the bleeding stopped and bandage on, and told me I would have nothing to worry about if I lay still for a couple of days. Nobody would tell the doctor anything. The police would not let him touch Morelli. He went away looking even more colourless and vague.

The big, sandy man had returned from the living-room holding one hand behind him. He waited until the doctor had gone, then asked: 'Have you got a pistol permit?'

'No.'

'Then what are you doing with this?' He brought from behind him the gun I had taken from Dorothy Wynant.

There was nothing I could say.

'You've heard about the Sullivan Act?' he asked.

'Yes.'

'Then you know where you stand. This gun yours?'

'No.'

'Whose is it?'

'I'll have to try to remember.'

He put the pistol in his pocket and sat down on a chair beside the bed. 'Listen, Mr Charles,' he said. 'I guess we're both of us doing this wrong. I don't want to get tough with you and I don't guess you really want to get tough with me. That hole in your side can't be making you feel any too good, so I ain't going to bother you any more till you've had a little rest. Then maybe we can get together the way we ought to.'

'Thanks,' I said and meant it. 'We'll buy a drink.'

Nora said: 'Sure,' and got up from the edge of the bed.

The big, sandy man watched her go out of the room. He shook his head solemnly. His voice was solemn: 'By God, sir, you're a lucky man.' He suddenly held out his hand. 'My name's Guild, John Guild.'

'You know mine.' We shook hands.

Nora came back with a siphon, a bottle of Scotch, and some glasses on a tray. She tried to give Morelli a drink, but Guild stopped her. 'It's mighty kind of you, Mrs Charles, but it's against the law to give a prisoner drinks or drugs except on a doctor's say-so.' He looked at me. 'Ain't that right?'

I said it was. The rest of us drank.

Presently Guild set down his empty glass and stood up. 'I got to take this gun along with me, but don't you worry about that. We got plenty of time to talk when you're feeling better.' He took Nora's hand and made an awkward bow over it. 'I hope you didn't mind what I said back there a while ago, but I meant it in a – '

Nora can smile very nicely. She gave him one of her nicest smiles. 'Mind? I liked it.'

She let the policemen and their prisoner out. Keyser had gone a few minutes before.

'He's sweet,' she said when she came back from the door. 'Hurt much?'

'No.'

'It's pretty much my fault, isn't it?'

'Nonsense. How about another drink?'

She poured me one. 'I wouldn't take too many of these today.'

'I won't,' I promised. 'I could do with some kippers for breakfast. And, now our troubles seem to be over for a while, you might have them send up our absentee watchdog. And tell the operator not to give us any calls; there'll probably be reporters.'

'What are you going to tell the police about Dorothy's pistol? You'll have to tell them something, won't you?'

'I don't know yet.'

'Tell me the truth, Nick: have I been too silly?'

I shook my head. 'Just silly enough.'

She laughed, said: 'You're a Greek louse,' and went around to the telephone.

IX

NORA said: 'You're just showing off, that's all it is. And what for? I know bullets bounce off you. You don't have to prove it to me.'

'It's not going to hurt me to get up.'

'And it's not going to hurt you to stay in bed at least one day. The doctor said – '

'If he knew anything he'd cure his own snuffles.' I sat up and put my feet on the floor. Asta tickled them with her tongue.

Nora brought me slippers and robe. 'All right, hard guy, get up and bleed on the rugs.'

I stood up cautiously and seemed to be all right as long as I went easy with my left arm and kept out of the way of Asta's front feet.

'Be reasonable,' I said. 'I didn't want to get mixed up with these people – still don't – but a fat lot of good that's doing me. Well, I can't just blunder out of it. I've got to see.'

'Let's go away,' she suggested. 'Let's go to Bermuda or Havana for a week or two, or back to the Coast.'

'I'd still have to tell the police some kind of story about that gun. And suppose it turns out to be the gun she was killed with? If they don't know already they're finding out.'

'Do you really think it is?'

'That's guessing. We'll go there for dinner tonight and – '

'We'll do nothing of the kind. Have you gone completely nuts? If you want to see anybody, have them come here.'

'It's not the same thing.' I put my arms around her. 'Stop worrying about this scratch. I'm all right.'

'You're showing off,' she said. 'You want to let people see you're a hero who can't be stopped by bullets.'

'Don't be nasty.'

'I will be nasty. I'm not going to have you – '

I shut her mouth with a hand over it. 'I want to see the Jorgensens together at home, I want to see Macaulay, and I want to see Studsy Burke. I've been pushed around too much. I've got to see about things.'

'You're so damned pig-headed,' she complained. 'Well, it's only five o'clock. Lie down till it's time to dress.'

I made myself comfortable on the living-room sofa. We had the afternoon papers sent up. Morelli, it seemed, had shot me – twice for one of the papers and three times for another – when I tried to arrest him for Julia Wolf's murder, and I was too near death to see anybody or to be moved to hospital. There were pictures of Morelli and a thirteen-year-old one of me in a pretty funny-looking hat, taken, I remembered, when I was working on the Wall Street explosion. Most of the follow-up stories on the murder of Julia Wolf were rather vague. We were reading them when our little constant visitor, Dorothy Wynant, arrived.

I could hear her at the door when Nora opened it: 'They wouldn't send my name up, so I sneaked up. Please don't send me away. I can help you nurse Nick. I'll do anything. Please, Nora.'

Nora had a chance then to say: 'Come on in.'

Dorothy came in. She goggled at me. 'B-but the papers said you – '

'Do I look like I'm dying? What's happened to you.' Her lower lip was swollen and cut near one corner, there was a bruise on one cheek-bone and two fingernail scratches down the other cheek, and her eyes were red and swollen.

'Mamma beat me,' she said. 'Look.' She dropped her coat on the floor, tore off a button unbuttoning her dress, took an arm out of its sleeve, and pushed the dress down to show her back. There were dark bruises on her arm, and her back was criss-crossed by long red welts. She was crying now. 'See?'

Nora put an arm around her. 'You poor kid.'

'What'd she beat you for?' I asked.

She turned from Nora and knelt on the floor beside my sofa. Asta came over and nuzzled her. 'She thought I came – came to see you about father and Julia Wolf.' Sobs broke up her sentences. 'That's why she came over here – to find out – and you made her think I didn't. You – you made her think you didn't care anything about what happened – just like you made me – and she was all right till she saw the papers this afternoon. Then she knew you'd been lying about not having anything to do with it. She beat me to try to make me tell her what I'd told you.'

'What'd you tell her?'

'I couldn't tell her anything. I – I couldn't tell her about Chris. I couldn't tell her anything.'

'Was he there?'

'Yes.'

'And he let her beat you like this?'

'But he – he never makes her stop.'

I said to Nora: 'For God's sake, let's have a drink.'

Nora said: 'Sure,' picked up Dorothy's coat, laid it across the back of a chair, and went into the pantry.

Dorothy said: 'Please let me stay here, Nick. I won't be any trouble, honestly, and you told me yourself I ought to walk out on them. You know you did, and I've got nowhere else to go. Please.'

'Take it easy. This thing needs a little figuring out. I'm as much afraid of Mimi as you are, you know. What did she think you'd told me?'

'She must know something – something about the murder

that she thinks I know – but I don't, Nick. Honest to God, I don't.'

'That helps a lot,' I complained. 'But listen, sister: there are things you know and we're going to start with those. You come clean at and from the beginning – or we don't play.'

She made a movement as if she were about to cross her heart. 'I swear I will,' she said.

'That'll be swell. Now let's drink.' We took a glass apiece from Nora. 'Tell her you were leaving for good?'

'No, I didn't say anything. Maybe she doesn't know yet I'm not in my room.'

'That helps some.'

'You're not going to make me go back?' she cried.

Nora said over her glass: 'The child can't stay and be beaten like that, Nick.'

I said: 'Sh-h-h. I don't know. I was just thinking that if we're going there for dinner maybe it's better for Mimi not to know – '

Dorothy stared at me with horrified eyes while Nora said: 'Don't think you're going to take me there now.'

Then Dorothy spoke rapidly: 'But Mamma doesn't expect you. I don't even know whether she'll be there. The papers said you were dying. She doesn't think you're coming.'

'So much the better,' I said. 'We'll surprise them.'

She put her face, white now, close to mine, spilling some of her drink on my sleeve in her excitement. 'Don't go. You can't go there now. Listen to me. Listen to Nora. You can't go.' She turned her white face around to look up at Nora. 'Can he? Tell him he can't.'

Nora, not shifting the focus of her dark eyes from my face, said: 'Wait, Dorothy. He ought to know what's best. What is it, Nick?'

I made a face at her. 'I'm just fumbling around. If you say Dorothy stays here, she stays. I guess she can sleep with Asta. But you've got to leave me alone on the rest of it. I don't know what I'm going to do because I don't know

37

what's being done to me. I've got to find out. I've got to find out in my own way.'

'We won't interfere,' Dorothy said. 'Will we, Nora?'

Nora continued to look at me, saying nothing.

I asked Dorothy: 'Where'd you get that gun? And nothing out of books this time.'

She moistened her lower lip and her face became pinker. She cleared her throat.

'Careful,' I said. 'If it's another piece of chewing-gum, I'll phone Mimi to come and get you.'

'Give her a chance,' Nora said.

Dorothy cleared her throat again. 'Can – can I tell you something that happened to me when I was a little child?'

'Has it got anything to do with the gun?'

'Not exactly, but it'll help you understand why I – '

'Not now. Some other time. Where'd you get the gun?'

'I wish you'd let me.' She hung her head.

'Where'd you get the gun?'

Her voice was barely audible. 'From a man in a speak-easy.'

I said: 'I knew we'd get the truth at last.' Nora frowned and shook her head at me. 'All right, say you did. What speakeasy?'

Dorothy raised her head. 'I don't know. It was on Tenth Avenue, I think. Your friend Mr Quinn would know. He took me there.'

'You met him after you left us that night?'

'Yes.'

'By accident, I suppose.'

She looked reproachfully at me. 'I'm trying to tell you the truth, Nick. I'd promised to meet him at a place called the Palma Club. He wrote the address down for me. So after I said good-night to you and Nora, I met him there and we went to a lot of places, winding up in this place where I got the gun. It was an awful tough place. You can ask him if I'm not telling the truth.'

'Quinn get the gun for you?'

'No. He'd passed out then. He was sleeping with his head on the table. I left him there. They said they'd get him home all right.'

'And the gun?'

'I'm coming to it.' She began to blush. 'He told me it was a gunman's hang-out. That's why I'd said let's go there. And after he went to sleep I got to talking to a man there, an awful tough-looking man. I was fascinated. And all the time I didn't want to go home, I wanted to come back here, but I didn't know if you'd let me.' Her face was quite red now and in her embarrassment she blurred her words. 'So I thought perhaps if I – if you thought I was in a terrible fix – and besides, that way I wouldn't feel so silly. Anyhow, I asked this awful tough-looking gangster, or whatever he was, if he would sell me a pistol or tell me where I could buy one. He thought I was kidding and laughed at first, but I told him I wasn't, and then he kept on grinning, but he said he'd see, and when he came back he said yes, he could get me one and asked how much I would pay for it. I didn't have much money, but I offered him my bracelet, but I guess he didn't think it was any good, because he said no, he'd have to have cash, so finally I gave him twelve dollars – all I had but a dollar for the taxi – and he gave me the pistol and I came over here and made up that about being afraid to go home because of Chris.' She finished so rapidly her words ran together, and she sighed as if very glad to have finished.

'Then Chris hasn't been making passes at you?'

She bit her lip. 'Yes, but not – not that bad.' She put both hands on my arms, and her face almost touched mine. 'You've got to believe me. I couldn't tell you all that, couldn't make myself out such a cheap little lying fool, if it wasn't the truth.'

'It makes more sense if I don't believe you,' I said. 'Twelve bucks isn't enough money. We'll let that rest for a minute, though. Did you know Mimi was going to see Julia Wolf that afternoon?'

'No. I didn't even know she was trying to find my father then. They didn't say where they were going that afternoon.'

'They?'

'Yes, Chris left the apartment with her.'

'What time was that?'

She wrinkled her forehead. 'It must've been pretty close to three o'clock – after two-thirty, anyway – because I remember I was late for a date to go shopping with Elsie Hamilton and was hurrying into my clothes.'

'They come back together?'

'I don't know. They were both home before I came.'

'What time was that?'

'Some time after six. Nick, you don't think they – Oh, I remember something she said while she was dressing. I don't know what Chris said, but she said: "When I ask her she'll tell me," in that Queen-of-France way she talks sometimes. You know. I didn't hear anything else. Does that mean anything?'

'What'd she tell you about the murder when you came home?'

'Oh, just about finding her and how upset she was and about the police and everything.'

'She seemed very shocked?'

Dorothy shook her head. 'No, just excited. You know Mamma.' She stared at me for a moment, asked slowly: 'You don't think she had anything to do with it?'

'What do you think?'

'I hadn't thought. I just thought about my father.' A little later she said gravely: 'If he did it, it's because he's crazy, but she'd kill somebody if she wanted to.'

'It doesn't have to be either of them,' I reminded her. 'The police seem to have picked Morelli. What'd she want to find your father for?'

'For money. We're broke: Chris spent it all.' She pulled down the corners of her mouth. 'I suppose we all helped, but he spent most of it. Mamma's afraid he'll leave her if she hasn't any money.'

'How do you know that?'

'I've heard them talk.'

'Do you think he will?'

She nodded with certainty. 'Unless she has money.'

I looked at my watch and said: 'The rest of it'll have to wait till we get back. You can stay here tonight, anyhow. Make yourself comfortable and have the restaurant send up your dinner. It's probably better if you don't go out.'

She stared miserably at me and said nothing.

Nora patted her shoulder. 'I don't know what he's doing, Dorothy, but if he says we ought to go there for dinner he probably knows what he's talking about. He wouldn't – '

Dorothy smiled and jumped up from the floor. 'I believe you. I won't be silly any more.'

I called the desk on the telephone and asked them to send up our mail. There were a couple of letters for Nora, one for me, some belated Christmas cards, a number of telephone-call memoranda slips, and a telegram from Philadelphia:

NICK CHARLES
THE NORMANDIE NEW YORK NY
WILL YOU COMMUNICATE WITH HERBERT MACAULAY TO
DISCUSS TAKING CHARGE OF INVESTIGATIONS OF WOLF
MURDER STOP AM GIVING HIM FULL INSTRUCTIONS STOP
BEST REGARDS

CLYDE MILLER WYNANT

I put the telegram in an envelope with a note saying it had just reached me and sent it by messenger to the Police Department Homicide Bureau.

X

In the taxicab Nora asked: 'You're sure you feel all right?'

'Sure.'

'And this isn't going to be too much for you?'

'I'm all right. What'd you think of the girl's story?'

She hesitated. 'You don't believe her, do you?'

'God forbid – at least till I've checked it up.'

'You know more about this kind of thing than I do,' she said, 'but I think she was at least trying to tell the truth.'

'A lot of the fancier yarns come from people who are trying to do that. It's not easy once you're out of the habit.'

She said: 'I bet you know a lot about human nature, Mr Charles. Now don't you? Sometimes you must tell me about your experiences as a detective.'

I said: 'Buying a gun for twelve bucks in a speakeasy. Well, maybe, but . . .'

We rode a couple of blocks in silence. Then Nora asked: 'What's really the matter with her?'

'Her old man's crazy: she thinks she is.'

'How do you know?'

'You asked me. I'm telling you.'

'You mean you're guessing?'

'I mean that's what's wrong with her; I don't know whether Wynant's actually nuts and I don't know whether she inherited any of it if he is, but she thinks both answers are yes, and it's got her doing figure eights.'

When we stopped in front of the Courtland she said: 'That's horrible, Nick. Somebody ought to – '

I said I didn't know: maybe Dorothy was right. 'Likely as not she's making doll clothes for Asta right now.'

We sent our names up to the Jorgensens and, after some delay, were told to go up. Mimi met us in the corridor when we stepped out of the elevator, met us with open arms and many words. 'Those wretched newspapers. They had me frantic with their nonsense about your being at death's door. I phoned twice, but they wouldn't give me your apartment, wouldn't tell me how you were.' She had both of my hands. 'I'm so glad, Nick, that it was just a pack of lies, even if you will have to take pot luck with us tonight. Naturally I didn't expect you and – But you're pale. You really have been hurt.'

42

'Not much,' I said. 'A bullet scraped my side, but it doesn't amount to anything.'

'And you came to dinner in spite of that! That is flattering, but I'm afraid it's foolish, too.' She turned to Nora. 'Are you sure it was wise to let him – '

'I'm not sure,' Nora said, 'but he wanted to come.'

'Men are such idiots,' Mimi said. She put an arm around me. 'They either make mountains out of nothing or utterly neglect things that may – But come in. Here, let me help you.'

'It's not that bad,' I assured her, but she insisted on leading me to a chair and packing me in with half a dozen cushions.

Jorgensen came in, shook hands with me, and said he was glad to find me more alive than the newspapers had said. He bowed over Nora's hand. 'If I may be excused one little minute more I will finish the cocktails.' He went out.

Mimi said: 'I don't know where Dorry is. Off sulking somewhere, I suppose. You haven't any children, have you?'

Nora said: 'No.'

'You're missing a lot, though they can be a great trial sometimes.' Mimi sighed. 'I suppose I'm not strict enough. When I do have to scold Dorry she seems to think I'm a complete monster.' Her face brightened. 'Here's my other tot. You remember Mr Charles, Gilbert. And this is Mrs Charles.'

Gilbert Wynant was two years younger than his sister, a gangling, pale, blond boy of eighteen with not too much chin under a somewhat slack mouth. The size of his remarkably clear blue eyes, and the length of the lashes, gave him a slightly effeminate look. I hoped he had stopped being the whining little nuisance he was as a kid.

Jorgensen brought in his cocktails, and Mimi insisted on being told about the shooting. I told her, making it even more meaningless than it had been.

43

'But why should he have come to you?' she asked.

'God knows. I'd like to know. The police'd like to know.'

Gilbert said: 'I read somewhere that when habitual criminals are accused of things they didn't do – even little things – they're much more upset by it than other people would be. Do you think that's so, Mr Charles?'

'It's likely.'

'Except,' Gilbert added, 'when it's something big, you know, something they would like to've done.'

I said again it was likely.

Mimi said: 'Don't be polite to Gil if he starts talking nonsense, Nick. His head's so cluttered up with reading. Get us another cocktail, darling.'

He went over to get the shaker. Nora and Jorgensen were in a corner sorting gramophone records.

I said: 'I had a wire from Wynant today.'

Mimi looked warily around the room, then leaned forward, and her voice was almost a whisper: 'What did he say?'

'Wanted me to find out who killed her. It was sent from Philadelphia this afternoon.'

She was breathing heavily. 'Are you going to do it?'

I shrugged. 'I turned it over to the police.'

Gilbert came back with the shaker. Jorgensen and Nora had put Bach's *Little Fugue* on the gramophone. Mimi quickly drank her cocktail and had Gilbert pour her another.

He sat down and said: 'I want to ask you: can you tell dope-addicts by looking at them?' He was trembling.

'Very seldom. Why?'

'I was wondering. Even if they're confirmed addicts?'

'The further along they are, the better the chances of noticing that something's wrong, but you can't often be sure it's dope.'

'Another thing,' he said. 'Gross says when you're stabbed you only feel a sort of push at the time and it's not until afterwards that it begins to hurt. Is that so?'

'Yes, if you're stabbed reasonably hard with a reasonably sharp knife. A bullet's the same way: you only feel the blow – and with a small-calibre, steel-jacketed bullet not much of that – at first. The rest comes when the air gets to it.'

Mimi drank her third cocktail and said: 'I think you're both being indecently gruesome, especially after what happened to Nick today. Do try to find Dorry, Gil. You must know some of her friends. Phone them. I suppose she'll be along presently, but I worry about her.'

'She's over at our place,' I said.

'At your place?' Her surprise may have been genuine.

'She came over this afternoon and asked if she could stay with us a while.'

She smiled tolerantly and shook her head. 'These youngsters!' She stopped smiling. 'A while?'

I nodded.

Gilbert, apparently waiting to ask me another question, showed no interest in this conversation between his mother and me.

Mimi smiled again and said: 'I'm sorry she's bothering you and your wife, but it's a relief to know she's there instead of off the Lord only knows where. She'll have finished her pouting by the time you get back. Send her along home, will you?' She poured me a cocktail. 'You've been awfully nice to her.'

I did not say anything.

Gilbert began: 'Mr Charles, do criminals – I mean professional criminals – usually – '

'Don't interrupt, Gil,' Mimi said. 'You will send her along home, won't you?' She was pleasant, but she was Dorothy's Queen-of-France.

'She can stay if she wants. Nora likes her.'

She shook a crooked finger at me. 'But I won't have you spoiling her like that. I suppose she told you all sorts of nonsense about me.'

'She did say something about a beating.'

45

'There you are,' Mimi said complacently, as if that proved her point. 'No, you'll have to send her home, Nick.'

I finished my cocktail.

'Well?' she asked.

'She can stay with us if she wants, Mimi. We like having her.'

'That's ridiculous. Her place is at home. I want her here.' Her voice was a little sharp. 'She's only a baby. You shouldn't encourage her foolish notions.'

'I'm not doing anything. If she wants to stay, she stays.'

Anger was a very pretty thing in Mimi's blue eyes. 'She's my child and she's a minor. You've been very kind to her, but this isn't being kind to her or to me, and I won't have it. If you won't send her home, I'll take steps to bring her home. I'd rather not be disagreeable about it, but' – she leaned forward and deliberately spaced her words – 'she's coming home.'

I said: 'You don't want to pick a fight with me, Mimi.'

She looked at me as if she were going to say I love you, and asked: 'Is that a threat?'

'All right,' I said, 'have me arrested for kidnapping, contributing to the delinquency of a minor, and mopery.'

She said suddenly in a harsh enraged voice: 'And tell your wife to stop pawing my husband.'

Nora, looking for another gramophone record with Jorgensen, had a hand on his sleeve. They turned to look at Mimi in surprise.

I said: 'Nora, Mrs Jorgensen wants you to keep your hands off Mr Jorgensen.'

'I'm awfully sorry.' Nora smiled at Mimi, then looked at me, put a very artificial expression of concern on her face, and in a somewhat sing-song voice, as if she were a school child reciting a piece, said: 'Oh, Nick, you're pale. I'm sure you have exceeded your strength and will have a relapse. I'm sorry, Mrs Jorgensen, but I think I should get him home and to bed right away. You will forgive us, won't you?'

Mimi said she would. Everybody was the soul of politeness to everybody else. We went downstairs and got a taxicab.

'Well,' Nora said, 'so you talked yourself out of a dinner. What do you want to do now? Go home and eat with Dorothy?'

I shook my head. 'I can do without Wynants for a little while. Let's go to Max's: I'd like some snails.'

'Right. Did you find out anything?'

'Nothing.'

She said meditatively: 'It's a shame that guy's so handsome.'

'What's he like?'

'Just a big doll. It's a shame.'

We had dinner and went back to the Normandie. Dorothy was not there. I felt as if I had expected that.

Nora went through the rooms, called up the desk. No note, no message had been left for us.

'So what?' she asked.

It was not quite ten o'clock. 'Maybe nothing,' I said. 'Maybe anything. My guess is she'll show up about three in the morning, tight, with a machine-gun she bought in Child's.'

Nora said: 'To hell with her. Get into pyjamas and lie down.'

XI

MY side felt a lot better when Nora called me at noon the next day. 'My nice policeman wants to see you,' she said. 'How do you feel?'

'Terrible. I must've gone to bed sober.' I pushed Asta out of the way and got up.

Guild rose with a drink in his hand when I entered the living-room, and smiled all across his broad, sandy face. 'Well, well, Mr Charles, you look spry enough this morning.'

I shook hands with him and said yes I felt pretty good, and we sat down.

He frowned good-naturedly. 'Just the same, you oughtn't've played that trick on me.'

'Trick?'

'Sure, running off to see people when I'd put off asking you questions to give you a chance to rest up. I kind of figured that ought to give me first call on you, as you might say.'

'I didn't think,' I said. 'I'm sorry. See that wire I got from Wynant?'

'Uh-huh. We're running it out in Philly.'

'Now about that gun,' I began, 'I – '

He stopped me. 'What gun? That ain't a gun any more. The firing pin's busted off, the guts are rusted and jammed. If anybody's fired it in six months – or could – I'm the Pope of Rome. Don't let's waste any time talking about that piece of junk.'

I laughed. 'That explains a lot. I took it away from a drunk who said he'd bought it in a speakeasy for twelve bucks. I believe him now.'

'Somebody'll sell him the City Hall one of these days. Man to man, Mr Charles, are you working on the Wolf job or ain't you?'

'You saw the wire from Wynant.'

'I did. Then you ain't working for him. I'm still asking you.'

'I'm not a private detective any more. I'm not any kind of a detective.'

'I heard that. I'm still asking you.'

'All right. No.'

He thought for a moment, said: 'Then let me put it another way: are you interested in the job?'

'I know the people, naturally I'm interested.'

'And that's all?'

'Yes.'

'And you don't expect to be working on it?'

The telephone rang and Nora went to answer it.

48

'To be honest with you, I don't know. If people keep on pushing me into it, I don't know how far they'll carry me.'

Guild wagged his head up and down. 'I can see that. I don't mind telling you I'd like to have you in on it – on the right side.'

'You mean not on Wynant's side. Did he do it?'

'That I couldn't say, Mr Charles, but I don't have to tell you he ain't helping us to find out who did it.'

Nora appeared in the doorway. 'Telephone, Nick.'

Herbert Macaulay was on the wire. 'Hello, Charles. How's the wounded?'

'I'm all right, thanks.'

'Did you hear from Wynant?'

'Yes.'

'I got a letter from him saying he had wired you. Are you too sick to – '

'No, I'm up and around. If you'll be in your office late this afternoon I'll drop in.'

'Swell,' he said. 'I'll be here till six.'

I returned to the living-room. Nora was inviting Guild to have lunch while we had breakfast. He said it was mighty kind of her. I said I ought to have a drink before breakfast. Nora went to order meals and pour drinks.

Guild shook his head and said: 'She's a mighty fine woman, Mr Charles.'

I nodded solemnly.

He said: 'Suppose you should get pushed into this thing, as you say, I'd like it a lot more to feel you were working with us than against us.'

'So would I.'

'That's a bargain then,' he said. He hunched his chair around a little. 'I don't guess you remember me, but back when you were working this town I was walking beat on Forty-third Street.'

'Of course,' I said, lying politely. 'I knew there was something familiar about – Being out of uniform makes a difference.'

'I guess it does. I'd like to be able to take it as a fact that you're not holding out anything we don't already know.'

'I don't mean to. I don't know what you know. I don't know very much. I haven't seen Macaulay since the murder and I haven't even been following it in the newspapers.'

The telephone was ringing again. Nora gave us our drinks and went to answer it.

'What we know ain't much of a secret,' Guild said, 'and if you want to take the time to listen I don't mind giving it to you.' He tasted his drink and nodded approvingly. 'Only there's a thing I'd like to ask first. When you went to Mrs Jorgensen's last night, did you tell her about getting the telegram from him?'

'Yes, and I told her I'd turned it over to you.'

'What'd she say?'

'Nothing. She asked questions. She's trying to find him.'

He put his head a little to one side and partly closed one eye. 'You don't think there's any chance of them being in cahoots, do you?' He held up a hand. 'Understand, I don't know why they would be or what it'd be all about if they were, but I'm just asking.'

'Anything's possible,' I said, 'but I'd say it was pretty safe they aren't working together. Why?'

'I guess you're right.' Then he added vaguely: 'But there's a couple of points.' He sighed. 'There always is. Well, Mr Charles, here's just about all we know for certain and if you can give us a little something more here and there as we go along I'll be mighty thankful to you.'

I said something about doing my best.

'Well, along about the 3rd of last October Wynant tells Macaulay he's got to leave town for a while. He don't tell Macaulay where he's going or what for, but Macaulay gets the idea that he's off to work on some invention or other that he wants to keep quiet – and he gets it out of Julia Wolf later that he's right – and he guesses Wynant's gone off to hide somewhere in the Adirondacks, but when he asks her about that later she says she don't know any more about it than he does.'

'She know what the invention was?'

Guild shook his head. 'Not according to Macaulay, only that it was probably something that he needed room for and machinery or things that cost money, because that's what he was fixing up with Macaulay. He was fixing it so Macaulay could get hold of his stocks and bonds and other things he owned and turn 'em into money when he wanted it and take care of his banking and everything just like Wynant himself.'

'Power of attorney covering everything, huh?'

'Exactly. And listen, when he wanted money, he wanted it in cash.'

'He was always full of screwy notions,' I said.

'That's what everybody says. The idea seems to be he don't want to take any chances on anybody tracing him through cheques, or anybody up there knowing he's Wynant. That's why he didn't take the girl along with him – didn't even let her know where he was, if she was telling the truth – and let his whiskers grow.' With his left hand he stroked an imaginary beard.

'"Up there",' I quoted. 'So he was in the Adirondacks?'

Guild moved one shoulder. 'I just said that because that and Philadelphia are the only ideas anybody's given us. We're trying the mountains, but we don't know. Maybe Australia.'

'And how much of this money in cash did Wynant want?'

'I can tell you that exactly.' He took a wad of soiled, bent and dog-eared papers out of his pocket, selected an envelope that was a shade dirtier than most of the others, and stuffed the others back in his pocket. 'The day after he talked to Macaulay he drew five thousand out of the bank himself, in cash. On the 28th – this is October, you understand – he had Macaulay get another five for him, and twenty-five hundred on the 6th of November, and a thousand on the 15th, and seventy-five hundred on the 30th, and fifteen hundred on the 6th – that would be December – and a thousand on the 18th, and five thousand on the 22nd, which was the day before she was killed.'

'Nearly thirty thou,' I said. 'A nice bank balance he had.'

'Twenty-eight thousand five hundred, to be exact.' Guild returned the envelope to his pocket. 'But, you understand, it wasn't all in there. After the first call Macaulay would sell something every time to raise the dough.' He felt in his pocket again. 'I got a list of the stuff he sold, if you want to see it.'

I said I didn't. 'How'd he turn the money over to Wynant?'

'Wynant would write the girl when he wanted it, and she'd get it from Macaulay. He's got her receipts.'

'And how'd she get it to Wynant?'

Guild shook his head. 'She told Macaulay she used to meet him places he told her, but he thinks she knew where he was, though she always said she didn't.'

'And maybe she still had that last five thousand on her when she was killed, huh?'

'Which might make it robbery, unless' – Guild's watery, grey eyes were almost shut – 'he killed her when he came there to get it.'

'Or unless,' I suggested, 'somebody else who killed her for some other reason, found the money there, and thought they might as well take it along.'

'Sure,' he agreed. 'Things like that happen all the time. It even happens sometimes that the first people that find a body like that pick up a little something before they turn in the alarm.' He held up a big hand. 'Of course, with Mrs Jorgensen – a lady like that – I hope you don't think I'm –'

'Besides,' I said, 'she wasn't alone, was she?'

'For a little while. The phone in the apartment was out of whack, and the elevator boy rode the superintendent down to phone from the office. But get me right on this,

I'm not saying Mrs Jorgensen did anything funny. A lady like that wouldn't be likely – '

'What was the matter with the phone?' I asked.

The door-bell rang.

'Well,' Guild said, 'I don't know just what to make of it. The phone had – '

He broke off as a waiter came in and began to set a table.

'About the phone,' Guild said when we were sitting at the table, 'I don't know just what to make of it, as I said. It had a bullet right smack through the mouthpiece of it.'

'Accidental or – ?'

'I'd just as lief ask you. It was from the same gun as the four that hit her, of course, but whether he missed her with that one or did it on purpose I don't know. It seems like a kind of noisy way to put a phone on the bum.'

'That reminds me,' I said, 'didn't anybody hear all this shooting? A ·32's not a shotgun, but somebody ought to've heard it.'

'Sure,' he said disgustedly. 'The place is lousy with people that think they hear things now, but nobody did anything about it then, and God knows they don't get together much on what they think they heard.'

'It's always like that,' I said sympathetically.

'Don't I know it.' He put a forkful of food in his mouth. 'Where was I? Oh, yes, about Wynant. He gave up his apartment when he went away, and put his stuff in storage. We been looking through it – the stuff – but ain't found anything yet to show where he went or even what he was working on, which we thought maybe might help. We didn't have any better luck in his shop on First Avenue. It's been locked up too since he went away, except that she used to go down there for an hour or two twice a week to take care of his mail and things. There's nothing to tell us anything in the mail that's come since she got knocked off. We didn't find anything in her place to help.' He smiled at Nora. 'I guess this must be pretty dull to you, Mrs Charles.'

'Dull?' She was surprised. 'I'm sitting on the edge of my chair.'

'Ladies usually like more colour,' he said, and coughed. 'Kind of glamour. Anyways, we got nothing to show where he's been, only he phones Macaulay last Friday and says to meet him at two o'clock in the Plaza lobby. Macaulay wasn't in, so he just left the message.'

'Macaulay was here,' I said, 'for lunch.'

'He told me. Well, Macaulay don't get to the Plaza till nearly three and he don't find any Wynant there and Wynant ain't registered there. He tried describing him, with and without a beard, but nobody at the Plaza remembers seeing him. He phones his office, but Wynant ain't called up again. And then he phones Julia Wolf and she tells him she don't even know Wynant's in town, which he figures is a lie, because he had just given her five thousand dollars for Wynant yesterday and figures Wynant's come for it, but he just says all right and hangs up and goes on about his business.'

'His business such as what?' I asked.

Guild stopped chewing the piece of roll he had just bitten off. 'I guess it wouldn't hurt to know, at that. I'll find out. There didn't seem to be anything pointing at him, so we didn't bother with that, but it don't ever hurt any to know who's got an alibi and who ain't.'

I shook my head no at the question he had decided not to ask. 'I don't see anything pointing at him, except that he's Wynant's lawyer and probably knows more than he's telling.'

'Sure. I understand. Well, that's what people have lawyers for, I guess. Now about the girl: maybe Julia Wolf wasn't her real name at all. We ain't been able to find out for sure yet, but we have found out she wasn't the kind of dame you'd expect him to be trusting to handle all that dough – I mean if he knew about her.'

'Had a record?'

He wagged a head up and down. 'This is elegant stew.

A couple of years before she went to work for him she did six months on a badger-game charge out West, in Cleveland, under the name of Rhoda Stewart.'

'You suppose Wynant knew that?'

'Search me. Don't look like he'd've turned her loose with that dough if he did, but you can't tell. They tell me he was kind of nuts about her, and you know how guys can go. She was running around off and on with this Shep Morelli and his boys too.'

'Have you really got anything on him?' I asked.

'Not on this,' he said regretfully, 'but we wanted him for a couple of other things.' He drew his sandy brows together a little. 'I wish I knew what sent him here to see you. Of course these junkies are likely to do anything, but I wish I knew.'

'I told you all I knew.'

'I'm not doubting that,' he assured me. He turned to Nora. 'I hope you don't think we were too rough with him, but you see you got to – '

Nora smiled and said she understood perfectly and filled his cup with coffee.

'Thank you, ma'am.'

'What's a junkie?' she asked.

'Hop-head.'

She looked at me. 'Was Morelli – ?'

'Primed to the ears,' I said.

'Why didn't you tell me?' she complained. 'I miss everything.' She left the table to answer the telephone.

Guild asked: 'You going to prosecute him for shooting you?'

'Not unless you need it.'

He shook his head. His voice was casual, though there was some curiosity in his eyes. 'I guess we got enough on him for a while.'

'You were telling me about the girl.'

'Yes,' he said. 'Well, we found out she's been spending a lot of nights away from her apartment – two or three

55

days at a stretch sometimes. Maybe that's when she was meeting Wynant. I don't know. We ain't been able to knock any holes in Morelli's story of not seeing her for three months. What do you make of that?'

'The same thing you do,' I replied. 'It's just about three months since Wynant went off. Maybe it means something, maybe not.'

Nora came in and said Harrison Quinn was on the telephone. He told me he had sold some bonds I was writing off losses on and gave me the prices.

'Have you seen Dorothy Wynant?' I asked.

'Not since I left her in your place, but I'm meeting her at the Palma for cocktails this afternoon. Come to think of it, she told me not to tell you. How about that gold, Nick? You're missing something if you don't get in on it. Those wild men from the West are going to give us some kind of inflation as soon as Congress meets, that's certain, and even if they don't, everybody expects them to. As I told you last week, there's already talk of a pool being – '

'All right,' I said, and gave him an order to buy some Dome Mines at 12.

He remembered then that he had seen something in the newspapers about my having been shot. He was pretty vague about it and paid very little attention to my assurances that I was all right. 'I suppose that means no ping-pong for a couple of days,' he said with what seemed genuine regret. 'Listen: you've got tickets for the opening tonight. If you can't use them I'll be – '

'We're going to use them. Thanks just the same.'

He laughed and said good-bye.

A waiter was carrying away the table when I returned to the living-room. Guild had made himself comfortable on the sofa. Nora was telling him: '. . . have to go away over the Christmas holidays every year because what's left of my family make a fuss over them and if we're home they come to visit us or we have to visit them, and Nick doesn't like it.' Asta was licking her paws in a corner.

Guild looked at his watch. 'I'm taking up a lot of you folks' time. I didn't mean to impose – '

I sat down and said: 'We were just about up to the murder, weren't we?'

'Just about.' He relaxed on the sofa again. 'That was on Friday the 23rd at some time before twenty minutes after three in the afternoon, which was the time Mrs Jorgensen got there and found her. It's kind of hard to say how long she'd been laying there dying before she was found. The only thing we know is that she was all right and answered the phone – and the phone was all right – at about half past two, when Mrs Jorgensen called her up, and was still all right around three, when Macaulay phoned.'

'I didn't know Mrs Jorgensen phoned.'

'It's a fact.' Guild cleared his throat. 'We didn't suspect anything there, you understand, but we checked it up just as a matter of course and found out from the girl at the switchboard at the Courtland that she put the call through for Mrs J. about two-thirty.'

'What did Mrs J. say?'

'She said she called up to ask where she could find Wynant, but this Julia Wolf said she didn't know, so Mrs J., thinking she's lying and maybe she can get her to tell the truth if she sees her, asked if she can drop in for a minute, and she says sure.' He frowned at my right knee. 'Well, she went there and found her. The apartment-house people don't remember seeing anybody going in or out of the Wolf apartment, but that's easy. A dozen people could do it without being seen. The gun wasn't there. There wasn't any signs of anybody busting in, and things in the place hadn't been disturbed any more than I've told you. I mean the place didn't look like it had been frisked. She had on a diamond ring that must've been worth a few hundred and there was thirty-some bucks in her bag. The people there know Wynant and Morelli – both of 'em have been in and out enough – but claim they ain't seen either for some time. The fire-escape window was locked and the

57

fire-escape didn't look like it had been walked on recently.'
He turned his hands over, palms up. 'I guess that's the
crop.'

'No fingerprints?'

'Hers, some belonging to the people that clean up the
place, near as we can figure. Nothing any good to us.'

'Nothing out of her friends?'

'She didn't seem to have any – not any close ones.'

'How about the – what was his name? – Nunheim who
identified her as a friend of Morelli's?'

'He just knew her by sight through seeing her around
with Morelli and recognized her picture when he saw it in
the paper.'

'Who is he?'

'He's all right. We know all about him.'

'You wouldn't hold out on me, would you,' I asked,
'after getting me to promise not to hold out on you?'

Guild said: 'Well, if it don't go any further, he's a fellow
that does some work for the department now and then.'

'Oh.'

He stood up. 'I hate to say it, but that's just about
as far as we've got. You got anything you can help
with?'

'No.'

He looked at me steadily for a moment. 'What do you
think of it?'

'That diamond ring, was it an engagement ring?'

'She had it on that finger.' After a pause he asked:
'Why?'

'It might help to know who bought it for her. I'm
going to see Macaulay this afternoon. If anything turns
up I'll give you a ring. It looks like Wynant, all right,
but – '

He growled good-naturedly: 'Uh-huh, but,' shook hands
with Nora and me, thanked us for our whisky, our lunch,
our hospitality, and our kindness in general, and went
away.

I told Nora: 'I'm not one to suggest that your charm wouldn't make any man turn himself inside out for you, but don't be too sure that guy isn't kidding us.'

'So it's come to that,' she said. 'You're jealous of policemen.'

XII

MACAULAY's letter from Clyde Wynant was quite a document. It was very badly typewritten on plain, white paper and dated Philadelphia, Pa., December 26, 1932. It read:

DEAR HERBERT:

I am telegraphing Nick Charles who worked for me you will remember some years ago and who is in New York to get in touch with you about the terrible death of poor Julia. I want you to do everything in your power to [a line had been x'd and m'd out here so that it was impossible to make anything at all of it] persuade him to find her murderer. I don't care what it costs – pay him!

Here are some facts I want you to give him outside of all you know about it yourself. I don't think he should tell these facts to the police, but he will know what is best and I want him to have a completely free hand as I have got the utmost confidence in him. Perhaps you had better just show him this letter, after which I must ask you to carefully destroy it.

Here are the facts.

When I met Julia Thursday night to get that $1,000 from her she told me she wanted to quit her job. She said she hadn't been at all well for some time and her doctor had told her she ought to go away and rest and now that her uncle's estate had been settled she could afford to and wanted to do it. She had never said anything about bad health before and I thought she was hiding her real reason and tried to get it out of her, but she stuck to what she had said. I didn't know anything about her uncle dying either. She said it was her Uncle John in Chicago. I suppose that could be looked up if it's important. I couldn't persuade her to change her mind, so she was to leave the last day of the month. She seemed worried or frightened, but she said she wasn't. I was sorry at first that she was going, but then I wasn't, because I had always been

59

able to trust her and now I wouldn't be if she was lying, as I thought she was.

The next fact I want Charles to know is that whatever anybody may think of whatever was true some time ago Julia and I ['are now' was x'd out lightly] were at the time of her murder *and had been for more than a year* not anything more to each other than employee and employer. This relationship was the result of mutual agreement.

Next, I believe some attempt should be made to learn the present whereabouts of the Victor Rosewater with whom we had trouble some years ago inasmuch as the experiments I am now engaged in are in line with those he claimed I cheated him out of and I consider him quite insane enough to have killed Julia in a rage at her refusal to tell him where I could be found.

Fourth, *and most important*, has my divorced wife been in communication with Rosewater? How did she learn I was carrying out experiments with which he once assisted me?

Fifth, the police must be convinced at once that I can tell them nothing about the murder so that they will take no steps to find me – steps that might lead to a discovery of and a premature exposure of my experiments, which I would consider *very dangerous* at this time. This can best be avoided by clearing up the mystery of her murder immediately, and that is what I wish to have done.

I will communicate with you from time to time and if in the meantime anything should arise to make communication with me *imperative* insert the following advertisement in the Times:

Abner. Yes. Bunny.

I will thereupon arrange to get in touch with you. I hope you sufficiently understand the necessity of persuading Charles to act for me, since he is already acquainted with the Rosewater trouble and knows most of the people concerned.

Yours truly,
CLYDE MILLER WYNANT

I put the letter down on Macaulay's desk and said: 'It makes a lot of sense. Do you remember what his row with Rosewater was about?'

'Something about changes in the structure of crystals. I can look it up.' Macaulay picked up the first sheet of the letter and frowned at it. 'He says he got a thousand dollars from her that night. I gave her five thousand for him; she told me that's what he wanted.'

'Four thousand from Uncle John's estate?' I suggested.

'Looks like it. That's funny: I never thought she'd gyp him. I'll have to find out about the other money I turned over to her.'

'Did you know she'd done a jail sentence in Cleveland on a badger-game charge?'

'No. Had she really?'

'According to the police – under the name of Rhoda Stewart. Where'd Wynant find her?'

He shook his head. 'I've no idea.'

'Know anything about where she came from originally, relatives, things like that?'

He shook his head again.

'Who was she engaged to?' I asked.

'I didn't know she was engaged.'

'She was wearing a diamond ring on that finger.'

'That's news to me,' he said. He shut his eyes and thought. 'No, I can't remember ever noticing an engagement ring.' He put his forearms on his desk and grinned over them at me. 'Well, what are the chances of getting you to do what he wants?'

'Slim.'

'I thought so.' He moved a hand to touch the letter. 'You know as much about how he feels as I do. What would make you change you mind?'

'I don't – '

'Would it help any if I could persuade him to meet you? Maybe if I told him that was the only way you'd take it – '

'I'm willing to talk to him,' I said, 'but he'd have to talk a lot straighter than he's writing.'

Macaulay asked slowly: 'You mean you think he may have killed her?'

'I don't know anything about that,' I said. 'I don't know as much as the police do, and it's a cinch they haven't got

61

enough on him to make the pinch even if they could find him.'

Macaulay sighed. 'Being a goof's lawyer is not much fun. I'll try to make him listen to reason, but I know he won't.'

'I meant to ask, how are his finances these days? Is he as well fixed as he used to be?'

'Almost. The depression's hurt him some, along with the rest of us, and the royalties from his smelting process have gone pretty much to hell now that the metals are dead, but he can still count on fifty or sixty thousand a year from his glassine and soundproofing patents, with a little more coming in from odds and ends like – ' He broke off to ask: 'You're not worrying about his ability to pay whatever you ask?'

'No, I was just wondering.' I thought of something else: 'Has he any relatives outside of his ex-wife and children?'

'A sister, Alice Wynant, that hasn't been on speaking terms with him for – it must be four or five years now.'

I supposed that was the Aunt Alice the Jorgensens had not gone to see Christmas afternoon. 'What'd they fall out about?' I asked.

'He gave an interview to one of the papers saying he didn't think the Russian Five Year Plan was necessarily doomed to failure. Actually he didn't make it much stronger than that.'

I laughed. 'They're a – '

'She's even better than he is. She can't remember things. The time her brother had his appendix out, she and Mimi were in a taxi going to see him the first afternoon and they passed a hearse coming from the direction of the hospital. Miss Alice turned pale and grabbed Mimi by the arm and said: "Oh dear! If that should be what's-his-name!"'

'Where does she live?'

'On Madison Avenue. It's in the phone book.' He hesitated. 'I don't think – '

'I'm not going to bother her.' Before I could say anything else his telephone began to ring.

He put the receiver to his ear and said: 'Hello. . . . Yes, speaking. . . . Who? . . . Oh, yes. . . .' Muscles tightened around his mouth, and his eyes opened a little wider. 'Where?' He listened some more. 'Yes, surely. Can I make it?' He looked at his watch on his left wrist. 'Right. See you on the train.' He put the telephone down. 'That was Lieutenant Guild,' he told me. 'Wynant's tried to commit suicide in Allentown, Pennsylvania.'

XIII

DOROTHY and Quinn were at the bar when I went into the Palma Club. They did not see me until I came up beside Dorothy and said: 'Hello, folks.' Dorothy had on the same clothes I had last seen her in.

She looked at me and at Quinn and her face flushed. 'You had to tell him.'

'The girl's in a pet,' Quinn said cheerfully. 'I got that stock for you. You ought to pick up some more and what are you drinking?'

'Old-fashioned. You're a swell guest – ducking out without leaving a word behind you.'

Dorothy looked at me again. The scratches on her face were pale, the bruise barely showed, and her mouth was no longer swollen. 'I trusted you,' she said. She seemed about to cry.

'What do you mean by that?'

'You know what I mean. Even when you went to dinner at Mamma's I trusted you.'

'And why not?'

Quinn said: 'She's been in a pet all afternoon. Don't bait her.' He put a hand on one of hers. 'There, there, darling, don't you – '

'Please shut up.' She took her hand away from him.

63

'You know very well what I mean,' she told me. 'You and Nora both made fun of me to Mamma and – '

I began to see what had happened. 'She told you that and you believed it?' I laughed. 'After twenty years you're still a sucker for her lies? I suppose she phoned you after we left: we had a row and didn't stay long.'

She hung her head and said: Oh, I am a fool,' in a low miserable voice: 'Listen, let's go over and see Nora now. I've got to square myself with her. I'm such an ass. It'd serve me right if she never – '

'Sure. There's plenty of time. Let's have this drink first.'

Quinn said: 'Brother Charles, I'd like to shake your hand. You've brought sunshine back into the life of our little tot and joy to – ' He emptied his glass. 'Let's go over and see Nora. The booze there is just as good and costs us less.'

'Why don't you stay here?' she asked him.

He laughed and shook his head. 'Not me. Maybe you can get Nick to stay here, but I'm going with you. I've put up with your snottiness all afternoon: now I'm going to bask in the sunshine.'

Gilbert Wynant was with Nora when we reached the Normandie. He kissed his sister and shook hands with me and, when he had been introduced, Harrison Quinn.

Dorothy immediately began to make long and earnest and none too coherent apologies to Nora.

Nora said: 'Stop it. There's nothing to forgive. If Nick's told you I was sore or hurt or anything of the sort he's just a Greek liar. Let me take your coat.'

Quinn turned on the radio. At the stroke of the gong it was five thirty-one and one quarter, Eastern Standard Time.

Nora told Quinn: 'Play bar-tender: you know where the stuff is,' and followed me into the bathroom. 'Where'd you find her?'

'In a speak. What's Gilbert doing here?'

'He came over to see her, so he said. She didn't go home

64

last night and he thought she was still here.' She laughed. 'He wasn't surprised at not finding her, though. He said she was always wandering off somewhere, she has dromo-mania, which comes from a mother-fixation, and is very interesting. He said Stekel claims people who have it usually show kleptomaniac impulses, too, and he's left things around to see if she'd steal them, but she never has yet that he knows of.'

'He's quite a lad. Did he say anything about his father?' 'No.'

'Maybe he hadn't heard. Wynant tried to commit suicide down in Allentown. Guild and Macaulay have gone down to see him. I don't know whether to tell the youngsters or not. I wonder if Mimi had a hand in his coming over here.'

'I wouldn't think so, but if you do – '

'I'm just wondering,' I said. 'Has he been here long?'

'About an hour. He's a funny kid. He's studying Chinese and writing a book on Knowledge and Belief – not in Chinese – and thinks Jack Oakie's very good.'

'So do I. Are you tight?'

'Not very.'

When we returned to the living-room, Dorothy and Quinn were dancing to *Eadie was a Lady*.

Gilbert put down the magazine he was looking at and politely said he hoped I was recovering from my injury.

I said I was.

'I've never been hurt, really hurt,' he went on, 'that I can remember. I've tried hurting myself, of course, but that's not the same thing. It just made me uncomfortable and irritable and sweat a lot.'

'That's pretty much the same thing,' I said.

'Really? I thought there'd be more – well, more to it.' He moved a little closer to me. 'It's things like that I don't know. I'm so horribly young I haven't had a chance to – Mr Charles, if you're too busy or don't want to, I hope you'll say so, but I'd appreciate it very much if you'd let me talk to you some time when there aren't a lot of people around to interrupt us. There are so many things I'd like to ask you, things I don't know anybody else could tell me and – '

'I'm not so sure about that,' I said, 'but I'll be glad to try any time you want.'

'You really don't mind? You're not just being polite?'

'No, I mean it, only I'm not sure you'll get as much help as you expect. It depends on what you want to know.'

'Well, things like cannibalism,' he said. 'I don't mean in places like Africa and New Guinea – in the United States, say. Is there much of it?'

'Not nowadays. Not that I know of.'

'Then there was once?'

'I don't know how much, but it happened now and then before the country was completely settled. Wait a minute: I'll give you a sample.' I went over to the bookcase and got the copy of Duke's *Celebrated Criminal Cases of America* that Nora had picked up in a second-hand book store, found the place I wanted, and gave it to him. 'It's only three or four pages.'

ALFRED G. PACKER, THE 'MANEATER', WHO MURDERED HIS FIVE COMPANIONS IN THE MOUNTAINS OF COLORADO, ATE THEIR BODIES AND STOLE THEIR MONEY.

'In the fall of 1873 a party of twenty daring men left Salt Lake City, Utah, to prospect in the San Juan country. Having heard glowing accounts of the fortunes to be made, they were light-hearted and full of hope as they started on their journey, but as the weeks rolled by and they beheld nothing but barren wastes and snowy mountains, they grew despondent. The farther they proceeded, the less inviting appeared the country, and they finally became desperate when it appeared that their only reward would be starvation and death.

'Just as the prospectors were about to give up in despair, they saw an Indian camp in the distance, and while they had no assurance as to what treatment they would receive at the hands of the "Reds", they decided that any death was preferable to starvation, so they agreed to take a chance.

'When they approached the camp they were met by an Indian who appeared to be friendly and escorted them to Chief Ouray. To their great surprise, the Indians treated them with every consideration and insisted upon their remaining in the camp until they had fully recuperated from their hardships.

'Finally the party decided to make another start, with the Los Pinos Agency as their goal. Ouray attempted to dissuade them from continuing the journey, and did succeed in influencing ten of the party to abandon the trip and return to Salt Lake. The other ten determined to continue, so Ouray supplied them with provisions and admonished them to follow the Gunnison River, which was named after Lieutenant Gunnison, who was murdered in 1852. (See life of Joe Smith, the Mormon.)

'Alfred G. Packer, who appeared as the leader of the party which continued the journey, boasted of his knowledge of the topography of the country and expressed confidence in his ability to find his way without difficulty. When his party had travelled a short distance, Packer told them that rich mines had recently been discovered near the headquarters of the Rio Grande River, and he offered to guide the party to the mines.

'Four of the party insisted that they follow Ouray's instructions, but Packer persuaded five men, named Swan, Miller, Noon, Bell and Humphrey, to accompany him to the mines, while the other four proceeded along the river.

'Of the party of four, two died from starvation and exposure, but the other two finally reached the Los Pinos Agency in February, 1874, after enduring indescribable hardships. General Adams was in command of this agency, and the unfortunate men were treated with every consideration. When they regained their strength they started back to civilization.

67

'In March, 1874, General Adams was called to Denver on business, and one cold, blizzardy morning, while he was still away, the employees of the agency, who were seated at the breakfast table, were startled by the appearance at the door of a wild-looking man who begged piteously for food and shelter. His face was frightfully bloated but otherwise he appeared to be in fairly good condition, although his stomach would not retain the food given him. He stated that his name was Packer and claimed that his five companions had deserted him while he was ill, but had left a rifle with him which he brought into the Agency.

'After partaking of the hospitality of the employees at the Agency for ten days, Packer proceeded to a place called Saquache, claiming that he intended to work his way to Pennsylvania, where he had a brother. At Saquache, Packer drank heavily and appeared to be well supplied with money. While intoxicated, he told many conflicting stories regarding the fate of his companions, and it was suspected that he had disposed of his erstwhile associates by foul means.

'At this time General Adams stopped at Saquache on his return from Denver to the Agency, and while at the home of Otto Mears he was advised to arrest Packer and investigate his movements. The General decided to take him back to the Agency, and while *en route* they stopped at the cabin of Major Downey, where they met the ten men who listened to the Indian chief and abandoned the trip. It was then proven that a great part of Packer's statement was false, so the General decided that the matter required a complete investigation, and Packer was bound and taken to the Agency, where he was held in close confinement.

'On April 2, 1874, two wildly excited Indians ran into the Agency, holding strips of flesh in their hands which they called "white man's meat", and which they stated they found just outside the Agency. As it had been lying on the snow and the weather had been extremely cold, it was still in good condition.

'When Packer caught sight of the exhibits, his face became livid, and with a low moan he sank to the floor. Restoratives were administered and after pleading for mercy, he made a statement substantially as follows:

'"When I and five others left Ouray's camp, we estimated that we had sufficient provisions for the long and arduous journey before us, but our food rapidly disappeared and we were soon on the verge of starvation. We dug roots from the ground upon which we subsisted for some days, but as they were not nutritious and as the extreme cold had driven all animals and birds to shelter, the situation became desperate. Strange looks came into the eyes of each of the party and they all became suspicious of each other. One day I went out to gather wood for the fire and when I returned I found that Mr Swan, the oldest man in the party, had been struck on the head and killed, and the remainder of the party were in the act of cutting up the body preparatory to eating it. His money, amounting to $2,000, was divided among the remainder of the party.

'"This food only lasted a few days, and I suggested that Miller be the next victim because of the large amount of flesh he carried. His skull was split open with a hatchet as he was in the act of picking up a piece of wood. Humphrey and Noon were the next victims. Bell and I then entered into a solemn compact that as we were the only ones left we would stand by each other whatever befell, and rather than harm each other we would die of starvation. One day Bell said: 'I can't stand it no longer,' and he rushed at me like a famished tiger, at the same time attempting to strike me with his gun. I parried the blow and killed him with a hatchet. I then cut his flesh into strips which I carried with me as I pursued my journey. When I espied the Agency from the top of the hill, I threw away the strips I had left, and I confess I did so reluctantly as I had grown fond of human flesh, especially that portion around the breast."

'After relating this gruesome story, Packer agreed to

69

guide a party in charge of H. Lauter to the remains of the murdered men. He led them to some high, inaccessible mountains, and as he claimed to be bewildered, it was decided to abandon the search and start back the next day.

'That night Packer and Lauter slept side by side, and during the night Packer assaulted him with the intent to commit murder and escape, but he was overpowered, bound, and after the party reached the Agency, he was turned over to the Sheriff.

'Early in June of that year, an artist named Reynolds, from Peoria, Ill., while sketching along the shores of Lake Christoval, discovered the remains of the five men lying in a grove of hemlocks. Four of the bodies were lying in a row, and the fifth, minus the head, was found a short distance away. The bodies of Bell, Swan, Humphreys and Noon had rifle bullet wounds in the back of the head, and when Miller's body was found it was crushed in, evidently by a blow from a rifle which was lying near by, the stock being broken from the barrel.

'The appearance of the bodies clearly indicated that Packer had been guilty of cannibalism as well as murder. He probably spoke the truth when he stated his preference for the breast of man, as in each instance the entire breast was cut away to the ribs.

'A beaten path was found leading from the bodies to a near-by cabin, where blankets and other articles belonging to the murdered men were discovered, and everything indicated that Packer lived in this cabin for many days after the murders, and that he made frequent trips to the bodies for his supply of human meat.

'After these discoveries the Sheriff procured warrants charging Packer with five murders, but during his absence the prisoner escaped.

'Nothing was heard of him again until January 29, 1883, nine years later, when General Adams received a letter from Cheyenne, Wyoming, in which a Salt Lake prospector stated that he had met Packer face to face in that locality.

The informant stated that the fugitive was known as John Schwartze, and was suspected of being engaged in operations with a gang of outlaws.

'Detectives began an investigation, and on March 12, 1883, Sheriff Sharpless of Laramie County arrested Packer, and on the 17th inst. Sheriff Smith of Hindale County brought the prisoner back to Lake City, Col.

'His trial on the charge of murdering Israel Swan in Hinsdale County on March 1, 1874, was begun on April 3, 1883. It was proven that each member of the party except Packer possessed considerable money. The defendant repeated his former statement, wherein he claimed that he had only killed Bell, and had done so in self-defence.

'On April 13, the jury found the defendant guilty with the death penalty attached. A stay of execution was granted to Packer, who immediately appealed to the Supreme Court. In the meantime he was transferred to the Gunnison jail to save him from mob violence.

'In October, 1885, the Supreme Court granted a new trial and it was then decided to bring him to trial on five charges of manslaughter. He was found guilty on each charge and was sentenced to serve eight years for each offence, making a total of forty years.

'He was pardoned on January 1, 1901, and died on a ranch near Denver on April 24, 1907.'

While Gilbert was reading this, I got myself a drink. Dorothy stopped dancing to join me. 'Do you like him?' she asked, jerking her head to indicate Quinn.

'He's all right.'

'Maybe, but he can be terribly silly. You didn't ask me where I stayed last night. Don't you care?'

'It's none of my business.'

'But I found out something for you.'

'What?'

'I stayed at Aunt Alice's. She's not exactly right in the

head, but she's awfully sweet. She told me she had a letter from my father today warning her against Mamma.'

'Warning her now? Just what did he say?'

'I didn't see it. Aunt Alice has been mad with him for several years and she tore it up. She says he's become a Communist and she's sure the Communists killed Julia Wolf and will kill him in the end. She thinks it's all over some secret they betrayed.'

I said: 'Oh my God!'

'Well, don't blame me. I'm just telling you what she told me. I told you she wasn't exactly right in the head.'

'Did she tell you that junk was in the letter?'

Dorothy shook her head. 'No. She only said the warning was. As near as I remember she said he wrote her not to trust Mamma under any circumstances and not to trust anybody connected with her, which I suppose means all of us.'

'Try to remember more.'

'But there wasn't any more. That's all she told me.'

'Where was the letter from?' I asked.

'She didn't know – except that it had come airmail. She said she wasn't interested.'

'What did she think of it? I mean, did she take the warning seriously?'

'She said he was a dangerous radical – they're her very words – and she wasn't interested in anything he had to say.'

'How seriously do you take it?'

She stared at me for a long moment and she moistened her lips before she spoke. 'I think he – '

Gilbert, book in hand, came over to us. He seemed disappointed in the story I had given him. 'It's very interesting,' he said, 'but if you know what I mean, it's not a pathological case.' He put an arm around his sister's waist. 'It was more a matter of that or starving.'

'Not unless you want to believe him,' I said.

Dorothy asked: 'What is it?'

'A thing in the book,' Gilbert replied.

'Tell him about the letter your aunt got,' I said to Dorothy.

She told him.

When she had finished, he grimaced impatiently. 'That's silly. Mamma's not really dangerous. She's just a case of arrested development. Most of us have outgrown ethics and morals and so on. Mamma's just not grown up to them yet.' He frowned and corrected himself thoughtfully: 'She might be dangerous, but it would be like a child playing with matches.'

Nora and Quinn were dancing.

'And what do you think of your father?' I asked.

Gilbert shrugged. 'I haven't seen him since I was a child. I've got a theory about him, but a lot of it's guesswork. I'd like – the chief thing I'd like to know is if he's impotent.'

I said: 'He tried to kill himself today, down in Allentown.'

Dorothy cried: 'He didn't,' so sharply that Quinn and Nora stopped dancing, and she turned and thrust her face up at her brother's. 'Where's Chris?' she demanded.

Gilbert looked from her face to mine and quickly back to hers. 'Don't be an ass,' he said coldly. 'He's off with that girl of his, that Fenton girl.'

Dorothy did not look as if she believed him.

'She's jealous of him,' he explained to me. 'It's that mother-fixation.'

I asked: 'Did either of you ever see the Victor Rosewater your father had trouble with back when I first knew you?'

Dorothy shook her head. Gilbert said: 'No. Why?'

'Just an idea I had. I never saw him either, but the description they gave me, with some easy changes, could be made to fit your Chris Jorgensen.'

XIV

THAT night Nora and I went to the opening of the Radio City Music Hall, decided we had had enough of the performance after an hour, and left. 'Where to?' Nora asked.

'I don't care. Want to hunt up that Pigiron Club that Morelli told us about? You'll like Studsy Burke. He used to be a safe-burglar. He claims to've cracked the safe in the Hagerstown jail while he was doing thirty days there for disorderly conduct.'

'Let's,' she said.

We went down to Forty-ninth Street and, after asking two taxi-drivers, two newsboys, and a policeman, found the place. The doorman said he didn't know about any Burkes, but he'd see. Studsy came to the door. 'How are you, Nick?' he said. 'Come on in.'

He was a powerfully built man of medium height, a little fat now, but not soft. He must have been at least fifty, but looked ten years younger than that. He had a broad, pleasantly ugly, pockmarked face under not much hair of no particular colour, and even his baldness could not make his forehead seem large. His voice was a deep bass growl.

I shook hands with him and introduced him to Nora.

'A wife,' he said. 'Think of that. By God, you'll drink champagne or you'll fight me.'

I said we wouldn't fight and we went inside. His place had a comfortably shabby look. It was between hours: there were only three customers in the place. We sat at a table in a corner and Studsy told the waiter exactly which bottle of wine to bring. Then he examined me carefully and nodded. 'Marriage done you good.' He scratched his chin. 'It's a long time I don't see you.'

'A long time,' I agreed.

'He sent me up the river,' he told Nora.

She clucked sympathetically. 'Was he a good detective?'

Studsy wrinkled what forehead he had. 'Folks say, but

I don't know. The once he caught me was a accident: I led with my right.'

'How come you sicked this wild man Morelli on me?' I asked.

'You know how foreigners are,' he said; 'they're hysterical. I don't know he's going to do nothing like that. He's worrying about the coppers trying to hang that Wolf dame's killing on him and we see in the paper you got something to do with it and I say to him: "Nick might not maybe sell his own mother out and you feel like you got to talk to somebody," so he says he will. What'd you do, make faces at him?'

'He let himself be spotted sneaking in and then blamed me for it. How'd he find me?'

'He's got friends and you wasn't hiding, was you?'

'I'd only been in town a week and there was nothing in the paper saying where I was staying.'

'Is that so?' Studsy asked with interest. 'Where you been?'

'I live in San Francisco now. How'd he find me?'

'That's a swell town. I ain't been there in years, but it's one swell town. I oughtn't to tell you, Nick. Ask him. It's his business.'

'Except that you sent him to me.'

'Well, yes,' he said, 'except that, of course; but then, see, I was putting in a boost for you.' He said it seriously.

I said: 'My pal.'

'How did I know he was going to blow his top? Anyways, he didn't hurt you much, did he?'

'Maybe not, but it didn't do me any good and I – ' I stopped as the waiter arrived with the champagne. We tasted it and said it was swell. It was pretty bad. 'Think he killed the girl?' I asked.

Studsy shook his head sidewise with certainty. 'No chance.'

'He's a fellow you can persuade to shoot,' I said.

'I know – these foreigners are hysterical – but he was around here all that afternoon.'

75

'All?'

'All. I'll take my oath to it. Some of the boys and girls were celebrating upstairs and I know for a fact he wasn't off his hip, let alone out of here, all afternoon. No kidding, that's a thing he can prove.'

'Then what was he worried about?'

'Do I know? Ain't that what I been asking him myself? But you know how these foreigners are.'

I said: 'Uh-huh. They're hysterical. He wouldn't't've sent a friend around to see her, would he?'

'I think you got the boy wrong,' Studsy said. 'I knew the dame. She used to come in here with him sometimes. They was just playing. He wasn't nuts enough about her that he'd have any reason for weighting her down like that. On the level.'

'Was she on the stuff, too?'

'I don't know. I seen her take it sometimes, but maybe she was just being sociable, taking a shot because he did.'

'Who else did she play around with?'

'Nobody I know,' Studsy replied indifferently. 'There was a rat named Nunheim used to come in here that was on the make for her, but he didn't get nowhere that I could see.'

'So that's where Morelli got my address.'

'Don't be silly. All Morelli'd want of him would be a crack at him. What's it to him telling the police Morelli knew the dame? A friend of yours?'

I thought it over and said: 'I don't know him. I hear he does chores for the police now and then.'

'M-m-m. Thanks.'

'Thanks for what? I haven't said anything.'

'Fair enough. Now you tell me something: what's all this fiddlededee about, huh? That guy Wynant killed her, didn't he?'

'A lot of people think so,' I said, 'but fifty bucks'll get you a hundred he didn't.'

He shook his head. 'I don't bet with you in your own

76

racket' – his face brightened – 'but I tell you what I will do and we can put some dough on it if you want. You know that time you copped me, I did lead with my right like I said, and I always wondered if you could do it again. Some time when you're feeling well I'd like – '

I laughed and said: 'No, I'm all out of condition.'

'I'm hog-fat myself,' he insisted.

'Besides that was a fluke: you were off balance and I was set.'

'You're just trying to let me down easy,' he said, and then more thoughtfully, 'though I guess you did get the breaks at that. Well, if you won't – Here, let me fill your glasses.'

Nora decided that she wanted to go home early and sober, so we left Studsy and his Pigiron Club at a little after eleven o'clock. He escorted us to a taxicab and shook our hands vigorously. 'This has been a fine pleasure,' he told us.

We said equally polite things and rode away.

Nora thought Studsy was marvellous. 'Half his sentences I can't understand at all.'

'He's all right.'

'You didn't tell him you'd quit gum-shoeing.'

'He'd've thought I was trying to put something over on him,' I explained. 'To a mug like him, once a sleuth always a sleuth, and I'd rather lie to him than have him think I'm lying. Have you got a cigarette? He really trusts me, in a way.'

'Were you telling the truth when you said Wynant didn't kill her?'

'I don't know. My guess is I was.'

At the Normandie there was a telegram for me from Macaulay in Allentown:

MAN HERE IS NOT WYNANT AND DID NOT TRY TO COMMIT SUICIDE.

XV

I HAD a stenographer in the next morning and got rid of
most of the mail that had been accumulating; had a telephone conversation with our lawyer in San Francisco – we
were trying to keep one of the mill's customers from being
thrown into bankruptcy; spent an hour going over a plan
we had for lowering our state taxes; was altogether the
busy business man, and felt pretty virtuous by two o'clock,
when I knocked off work for the day and went out to lunch
with Nora.

She had a date to play bridge after lunch. I went down
to see Guild: I had talked to him on the telephone earlier in
the day.

'So it was a false alarm?' I said after we had shaken
hands and made ourselves comfortable in chairs.

'That's what it was. He wasn't any more Wynant than
I am. You know how it is: we told the Philly police he'd
sent a wire from there and broadcasted his description, and
for the next week anybody that's skinny and maybe got
whiskers is Wynant to half of the State of Pennsylvania.
This was a fellow named Barlow, a carpenter out of work
as near as we can figure out, that got hot by a nigger trying to stick him up. He can't talk much yet.'

'He couldn't've been shot by somebody who made the
same mistake the Allentown police did?' I asked.

'You mean thought he was Wynant? I guess that could
be – if it helps any. Does it?'

I said I didn't know. 'Did Macaulay tell you about the
letter he got from Wynant?'

'He didn't tell me what was in it.'

I told him. I told him what I knew about Rosewater.

He said: 'Now, that's interesting.'

I told him about the letter Wynant had sent his sister.

He said: 'He writes a lot of people, don't he?'

'I thought of that.' I told him Victor Rosewater's description with a few easy changes would fit Christian Jorgensen.

He said: 'It don't hurt any to listen to a man like you. Don't let me stop you.'

I told him that was the crop.

He rocked back in his chair and screwed his pale grey eyes up at the ceiling. 'There's some work to be done there,' he said presently.

'Was this fellow in Allentown shot with a ·32?' I asked.

Guild stared curiously at me for a moment, then shook his head. 'A ·44. You got something on your mind?'

'No. Just chasing the set-up around in my head.'

He said: 'I know what that is,' and leaned back to look at the ceiling some more. When he spoke again it was as if he was thinking of something else. 'That alibi of Mac-aulay's you was asking about is all right. He was late for a date then and we know for a fact he was in a fellow's office named Hermann on Fifty-seventh Street from five minutes after three till twenty after, the time that counts.'

'What's the five minutes after three?'

'That's right, you don't know about that. Well, we found a fellow named Caress with a cleaning and dyeing place on First Avenue that called her up at five minutes after three to ask her if she had any work for him, and she said no and told him she was liable to go away. So that narrows the time down to from three five to three twenty. You ain't really suspicious of Macaulay?'

'I'm suspicious of everybody,' I said. 'Where were you between three five and three twenty?'

He laughed. 'As a matter of fact,' he said, 'I'm just about the only one of the lot that ain't got an alibi. I was at the moving pictures.'

'The rest of them have?'

He wagged his head up and down. 'Jorgensen left his place with Mrs Jorgensen – that was about five minutes to three – and sneaked over on West Seventy-third Street to see a girl named Olga Fenton – we promised not to tell his wife – and stayed there till about five. We know what Mrs

79

Jorgensen did. The daughter was dressing when they left and she took a taxi at a quarter past and went straight to Bergdorf-Goodman's. The son was in the Public Library all afternoon – God, he reads funny books. Morelli was in a joint over in the Forties.' He laughed. 'And where was you?'

'I'm saving mine till I really need it. None of those look too air-tight, but legitimate alibis seldom do. How about Nunheim?'

Guild seemed surprised. 'What makes you think of him?'

'I hear he had a yen for the girl.'

'And where'd you hear it?'

'I heard it.'

He scowled. 'Would you say it was reliable?'

'Yes.'

'Well,' he said slowly, 'he's one guy we can check up on. But look here, what do you care about these people? Don't you think Wynant done it?'

I gave him the same odds I had given Studsy: 'Twenty-five'll get you fifty he didn't.'

He scowled at me over that for a long silent moment, then said: 'That's an idea, anyways. Who's your candidate?'

'I haven't got that far yet. Understand, I don't know anything. I'm not saying Wynant didn't do it. I'm just saying everything doesn't point at him.'

'And saying it two to one. What don't point at him?'

'Call it a hunch, if you want,' I said, 'but – '

'I don't want to call it anything,' he said. 'I think you're a smart detective. I want to listen to what you got to say.'

'Mostly I've got questions to say. For instance, how long was it from the time the elevator boy let Mrs Jorgensen off at the Wolf girl's floor until she rang for him and said she heard groans?'

Guild pursed his lips, opened them to ask: 'You think she might've – ?' and left the rest of the question hanging in the air.

'I think she might've. I'd like to know where Nunheim was. I'd like to know the answers to the questions in Wynant's letter. I'd like to know where the four-thousand-dollar difference between what Macaulay gave the girl and what she seems to have given Wynant went. I'd like to know where her engagement ring came from.'

'We're doing the best we can,' Guild said. 'Me – just now I'd like to know why, if he didn't do it, Wynant don't come in and answer questions for us.'

'One reason might be that Mrs Jorgensen'd like to slam him in the squirrel cage again.' I thought of something. 'Herbert Macaulay's working for Wynant: you didn't just take Macaulay's word for it that the man in Allentown wasn't him?'

'No. He was a younger man than Wynant, with damned little grey in his hair and no dye, and he didn't look like the pictures we got.' He seemed positive. 'You got anything to do the next hour or so?'

'No.'

'That's fine.' He stood up. 'I'll get some of the boys working on these things we been discussing and then may-be me and you will pay some visits.'

'Swell,' I said, and went out of the office.

There was a copy of the *Times* in his waste-basket. I fished it out and turned to the Public Notices columns. Macaulay's advertisement was there:

'*Abner. Yes. Bunny.*'

When Guild returned I asked: 'How about Wynant's help, whoever he had working in the shop? Have they been looked up?'

'Uh-huh, but they don't know anything. They was laid off at the end of the week that he went away – there's two of them – and haven't seen him since.'

'What were they working on when the shop was closed?'

'Some kind of paint or something – something about a permanent green. I don't know. I'll find out if you want.'

'I don't suppose it matters. Is it much of a shop?'

81

'Looks like a pretty good lay-out, far as I can tell. You think the shop might have something to do with it?'

'Anything might.'

'Uh-huh. Well, let's run along.'

XVI

'First thing,' Guild said as we left his office, 'we'll go see Mr Nunheim. He ought to be home: I told him to stick around till I phoned him.'

Mr Nunheim's home was on the fourth floor of a dark, damp, and smelly building made noisy by the Sixth Avenue elevated. Guild knocked on the door.

There were sounds of hurried movements inside, then a voice asked: 'Who is it?' The voice was a man's, nasal, somewhat irritable.

Guild said 'John.'

The door was hastily opened by a small, sallow man of thirty-five or -six whose visible clothes were an undershirt, blue pants, and black silk stockings. 'I wasn't expecting you, Lieutenant,' he whined. 'You said you'd phone.' He seemed frightened. His dark eyes were small and set close together; his mouth was wide, thin, and loose; and his nose was peculiarly limber, a long, drooping nose, apparently boneless.

Guild touched my elbow with his hand and we went in. Through an open door to the left an unmade bed could be seen. The room we entered was a living-room, shabby and dirty, with clothing, newspapers, and dirty dishes sitting around. In an alcove to the right there was a sink and a stove. A woman stood between them holding a sizzling skillet in her hand. She was a big-boned, full-fleshed, red-haired woman of perhaps twenty-eight, handsome in a rather brutal, sloppy way. She wore a rumpled pink kimono and frayed pink mules with lopsided bows on them. She stared sullenly at us.

Guild did not introduce me to Nunheim and he paid no attention to the woman. 'Sit down,' he said, and pushed some clothing out of the way to make a place for himself on an end of the sofa.

I removed part of a newspaper from a rocking-chair and sat down. Since Guild kept his hat on I did the same with mine.

Nunheim went over to the table, where there was about two inches of whisky in a pint bottle and a couple of tumblers, and said: 'Have a shot?'

Guild made a face. 'Not that vomit. What's the idea of telling me you just knew the Wolf girl by sight?'

'That's all I did, Lieutenant, that's the truth.' Twice his eyes slid sidewise towards me and he jerked them back. 'Maybe I said hello to her, or how are you or something like that when I saw her, but that's all I knew her. That's the truth.'

The woman in the alcove laughed, once, derisively, and there was no merriment in her face.

Nunheim twisted himself around to face her. 'All right,' he told her, his voice shrill with rage, 'put your mouth in and I'll pop a tooth out of it.'

She swung her arm and let the skillet go at his head. It missed, crashing into the wall. Grease and egg-yolks made fresher stains on wall, floor, and furniture.

He started for her. I did not have to rise to put out a foot and trip him. He tumbled down on the floor. The woman had picked up a paring knife.

'Cut it out,' Guild growled. He had not stood up either. 'We come here to talk to you, not to watch this rough-house comedy. Get up and behave yourself.'

Nunheim got slowly to his feet. 'She drives me nuts when she's drinking,' he said. 'She's been ragging me all day.' He moved his right hand back and forth. 'I think I sprained my wrist.'

The woman walked past us without looking at any of us, went into the bedroom, and shut the door.

Guild said: 'Maybe if you'd quit sucking around after other women you wouldn't have so much trouble with this one.'

'What do you mean, Lieutenant?' Nunheim was surprised and innocent and perhaps pained.

'Julia Wolf.'

The little sallow man was indignant now. 'That's a lie, Lieutenant. Anybody that says I ever – '

Guild interrupted him by addressing me: 'If you want to take a poke at him, I wouldn't stop on account of his bum wrist: he couldn't even hit hard anyhow.'

Nunheim turned to me with both hands out. 'I didn't mean you were a liar. I meant maybe somebody made a mistake if they – '

Guild interrupted him again: 'You wouldn't've taken her if you could've got her?'

Nunheim moistened his lower lip and looked warily at the bedroom door. 'Well,' he said slowly in a cautiously low voice, 'of course she was a classy number. I guess I wouldn't've turned it down.'

'But you never tried to make her?'

Nunheim hesitated, then moved his shoulders and said: 'You know how it is. A fellow knocking around tries 'most everything he runs into.'

Guild looked sourly at him. 'You'd done better to tell me that in the beginning. Where were you the afternoon she was knocked off?'

The little man jumped as if he had been stuck with a pin. 'For Christ's sake, Lieutenant, you don't think I had anything to do with that. What would I want to hurt her for?'

'Where were you?'

Nunheim's loose lips twitched nervously. 'What day was she – ' He broke off as the bedroom door opened.

The big woman came out carrying a suitcase. She had put on street clothes.

'Miriam,' Nunheim said.

She stared at him dully and said: 'I don't like crooks,

and even if I did, I wouldn't like crooks that are stool-pigeons, and if I liked crooks that are stool-pigeons, I still wouldn't like you.' She turned to the outer door.

Guild, catching Nunheim's arms to keep him from following the woman, repeated: 'Where were you?'

Nunheim called: 'Miriam. Don't go. I'll behave, I'll do anything. Don't go, Miriam.'

She went out and shut the door.

'Let me go,' he begged Guild. 'Let me bring her back. I can't get along without her. I'll bring her right back and tell you anything you want to know. Let me go. I've got to have her.'

Guild said: 'Nuts. Sit down.' He pushed the little man down in a chair. 'We didn't come here to watch you and that broad dance around a maypole. Where were you the afternoon the girl was killed?'

Nunheim put his hands over his face and began to cry.

'Keep on stalling,' Guild said, 'and I'm going to slap you silly.'

I poured some whisky in a tumbler and gave it to Nunheim.

'Thank you, sir, thank you.' He drank it, coughed, and brought out a dirty handkerchief to wipe his face with. 'I can't remember off-hand, Lieutenant,' he whined. 'Maybe I was over at Charlie's shooting pool, maybe I was here. Miriam would remember if you'll let me go bring her back.'

Guild said: 'The hell with Miriam. How'd you like to be thrown in the can on account of not remembering?'

'Just give me a minute. I'll remember. I'm not stalling, Lieutenant. You know I always come clean with you. I'm just upset now. Look at my wrist.' He held up his right wrist to let us see it was swelling. 'Just one minute.' He put his hands over his face again.

Guild winked at me and we waited for the little man's memory to work.

Suddenly he took his hands down from his face and laughed. 'Holy hell! It would serve me right if you had pinched me. That's the afternoon I was – Wait, I'll show you.' He went into the bedroom.

After a few minutes Guild called: 'Hey, we haven't got all night. Shake it up.'

There was no answer.

The bedroom was empty when we went into it, and when we opened the bathroom door the bathroom was empty. There was an open window and a fire-escape.

I said nothing, tried to look nothing.

Guild pushed his hat back a little from his forehead and said: 'I wish he hadn't done that.' He went to the telephone in the living-room.

Whilst he was telephoning, I poked around in drawers and closets, but found nothing. My search was not very thorough and I gave it up as soon as he finished putting the police machinery in action.

'I guess we'll find him all right,' he said. 'I got some news. We've identified Jorgensen as Rosewater.'

'Who made the identification?'

'I sent a man over to talk to the girl that gave him his alibi, this Olga Felton, and he finally got it out of her. He says he couldn't shake her on the alibi, though. I'm going over and have a try at her. Want to come along?'

I looked at my watch and said: 'I'd like to, but it's too late. Picked him up yet?'

'The order's out.' He looked thoughtfully at me. 'And will that baby have to do some talking!'

I grinned at him. 'Now who do you think killed her?'

'I'm not worrying,' he said. 'Just let me have things to squeeze enough people with and I'll turn up the right one before the whistle blows.'

In the street he promised to let me know what happened, and we shook hands and separated. He ran after me a couple of seconds later to send his very best regards to Nora.

XVII

HOME, I delivered Guild's message to Nora and told her
the day's news.

'I've got a message for you, too,' she said. 'Gilbert
Wynant dropped in and was quite disappointed at missing
you. He asked me to tell you he has something of the
"utmost importance" to tell you.'

'He's probably discovered that Jorgensen has a mother-
fixation.'

'Do you think Jorgensen killed her?' she asked.

'I thought I knew who did it,' I said, 'but it's too mixed
up right now for anything but guesses.'

'And what's your guess?'

'Mimi, Jorgensen, Wynant, Nunheim, Gilbert, Dorothy,
Aunt Alice, Morelli, you, me, or Guild. Maybe Studsy did
it. How about shaking up a drink?'

She mixed some cocktails. I was on my second or third
when she came back from answering the telephone and
said: 'Your friend Mimi wants to talk to you.'

I went to the telephone. 'Hello, Mimi.'

'I'm awfully sorry I was so rude the other night, Nick,
but I was so upset and I just simply lost my temper and
made a show of myself. Please forgive me.' She ran through
this very rapidly, as if anxious to get it over with.

'That's all right,' I said.

She hardly let me get me three words out before she was
speaking again, but slower and more earnestly now: 'Can
I see you, Nick? Something horrible has happened, something – I don't know what to do, which way to turn.'

'What is it?'

'I can't tell you over the phone, but you've got to tell
me what to do. I've got to have somebody's advice. Can't
you come over?'

'You mean now?'

'Yes. Please.'

I said: 'All right,' and went back to the living-room. 'I'm going to run over and see Mimi. She says she's in a jam and needs help.'

Nora laughed. 'Keep your legs crossed. She apologize to you? She did to me.'

'Yes, all in one breath. Is Dorothy home or still at Aunt Alice's?'

'Still at Auntie's, according to Gilbert. How long will you be?'

'No longer than I have to. The chances are they've copped Jorgensen and she wants to know if it can be fixed.'

'Can they do anything to him? I mean if he didn't kill the Wolf girl.'

'I suppose the old charges against him – threats by mail, attempted extortion – could be raked up.' I stopped drinking to ask Nora and myself a question: 'I wonder if he and Nunheim know each other.' I thought that over, but could make nothing more than a possibility of it. 'Well, I'm on my way.'

XVIII

MIMI received me with both hands. 'It's awfully, awfully nice of you to forgive me, Nick, but then you've always been awfully nice. I don't know what got into me Monday night.'

I said: 'Forget it.'

Her face was somewhat pinker than usual and the firmness of its muscles made it seem younger. Her blue eyes were very bright. Her hands had been cold on mine. She was tense with excitement, but I could not figure out what kind of excitement it was.

She said: 'It was awfully sweet of your wife, too, to – '

'Forget it.'

'Nick, what can they do to you for concealing evidence that somebody's guilty of a murder?'

'Make you an accomplice – accomplice after the fact is the technical term – if they want.'

'Even if you voluntarily change your mind and give them the evidence?'

'They can. Usually they don't.'

She looked around the room as if to make sure there was nobody else there and said: 'Clyde killed Julia. I found the proof and hid it. What'll they do to me?'

'Probably nothing except give you hell – if you turn it in. He was once your husband: you and he are close enough together that no jury'd be likely to blame you for trying to cover him up – unless, of course, they had reason to think you had some other motive.'

She asked coolly, deliberately: 'Do you?'

'I don't know,' I said. 'My guess would be that you had intended to use this proof of his guilt to shake him down for some dough as soon as you could get in touch with him, and that now something else has come up to make you change your mind.'

She made a claw of her right hand and struck at my face with her pointed nails. Her teeth were together, her lips drawn far back over them.

I caught her wrist. 'Women are getting tough,' I said, trying to sound wistful. 'I just left one that heaved a skillet at a guy.'

She laughed, though her eyes did not change. 'You always think the worst of me, don't you?'

I took my hand away from her wrist and she rubbed the marks my finger had left on it.

'Who was the woman who threw the skillet?' she asked. 'Anyone I know?'

'It wasn't Nora, if that's what you mean. Have they arrested Victor-Christian Rosewater-Jorgensen yet?'

'What?'

I believed in her bewilderment, though both it and my belief in it surprised me. 'Jorgensen is Rosewater,' I said. 'You remember him. I thought you knew.'

'You mean that horrible man who – ?'

'Yes.'

'I won't believe it.' She stood up working her fingers together. 'I won't. I won't.' Her face was sick with fear, her voice strained, unreal as a ventriloquist's. 'I won't believe it.'

'That'll help a lot,' I said.

She was not listening to me. She turned her back to me and went to a window, where she stood with her back to me.

I said: 'There's a couple of men in a car out front who look like they might be coppers waiting to pick him up when he – '

She turned around and asked sharply: 'Are you sure he's Rosewater?' Most of the fear had already gone out of her face and her voice was at least human again.

'The police are.'

We stared at each other, both of us busy thinking. I was thinking she had not been afraid that Jorgensen killed Julia Wolf, or even that he might be arrested: she was afraid his only reason for marrying her had been as a move in some plot against Wynant.

When I laughed – not because the idea was funny, but because it had come to me so suddenly – she started and smiled uncertainly. 'I won't believe it,' she said, and her voice was very soft now, 'until he tells me himself.'

'And when he does – then what?'

She moved her shoulders a little, and her lower lip quivered. 'He is my husband.'

That should have been funny, but it annoyed me. I said: 'Mimi, this is Nick. You remember me, N-i-c-k.'

'I know you never think any good of me,' she said gravely. 'You think I'm – '

'All right. All right. Let it pass. Let's get back to the dope on Wynant you found.'

'Yes, that,' she said, and turned away from me. When

she turned back her lip was quivering again. 'That was a lie, Nick, I didn't find anything.' She came close to me. 'Clyde had·no right to send those letters to Alice and Macaulay trying to make everybody suspicious of me and I thought it would serve him right if I made up something against him, because I really did think – I mean, I do think – he killed her and it was only – '

'What'd you make up?' I asked.

'I – I hadn't made it up yet. I wanted to find out about what they could do – you know, the things I asked you – first. I might've pretended she came to a little when I was alone with her, while the others were phoning, and told me he did it.'

'You didn't say you heard something and kept quiet, you said you found something and hid it.'

'But I hadn't really made up my mind what I – '

'When'd you hear about Wynant's letter to Macaulay?'

'This afternoon,' she said; 'there was a man here from the police.'

'Didn't he ask you anything about Rosewater?'

'He asked me if I knew him or had ever known him, and I thought I was telling the truth when I said no.'

'Maybe you did,' I said, 'and for the first time I now believe you were telling the truth when you said you found some sort of evidence against Wynant.'

She opened her eyes wider. 'I don't understand.'

'Neither do I, but it could be like this: you could've found something and decided to hold it out, probably with the idea of selling it to Wynant; then when his letters started people looking you over, you decided to give up the money idea and both pay him back and protect yourself by turning it over to the police; and, finally, when you learn that Jorgensen is Rosewater, you make another about-face and hold it out, not for money this time, but to leave Jorgensen in as bad a spot as possible as punishment for having married you as a trick in his game against Wynant and not for love.'

She smiled calmly and asked: 'You really think me to be capable of anything, don't you?'

'That doesn't matter,' I said. 'What ought to matter to you is that you'll probably wind up your life in prison somewhere.'

Her scream was not loud, but it was horrible, and the fear that had been in her face before was as nothing to that there now. She caught my lapels and clung to them, babbling: 'Don't say that, please don't. Say you don't think it.' She was trembling so I put an arm around her to keep her from falling.

We did not hear Gilbert until he coughed and asked: 'Aren't you well, Mamma?'

She slowly took her hands down from my lapels and moved back a step and said: 'Your mother's a silly woman.' She was still trembling, but she smiled at me and she made her voice playful: 'You're a brute to frighten me like that.'

I said I was sorry.

Gilbert put his coat and hat on a chair and looked from one to the other of us with polite interest. When it became obvious that neither of us was going to tell him anything he coughed again, said: 'I'm awfully glad to see you,' and came over to shake hands with me.

I said I was glad to see him.

Mimi said: 'Your eyes look tired. I bet you've been reading all afternoon without your glasses again.' She shook her head and told me: 'He's as unreasonable as his father.'

'Is there any news of Father?' he asked.

'Not since that false alarm about his suicide,' I said. 'I suppose you heard it was a false alarm.'

'Yes.' He hesitated. 'I'd like to see you for a few minutes before you go.'

'Sure.'

'But you're seeing him now, darling,' Mimi said. 'Are there secrets between you that I'm not supposed to know about?' Her tone was light enough. She had stopped trembling.

'It would bore you.' He picked up his hat and coat, nodded at me, and left the room.

Mimi shook her head again and said: 'I don't understand that child at all. I wonder what he made of our tableau.' She did not seem especially worried. Then, more seriously. 'What made you say that, Nick?'

'About you winding up in – ?'

'No, never mind.' She shuddered. 'I don't want to hear it. Can't you stay for dinner? I'll probably be all alone.'

'I'm sorry I can't. Now how about this evidence you found.'

'I didn't really find anything. That was a lie.' She frowned earnestly. 'Don't look at me like that. It really was a lie.'

'So you sent for me just to lie to me?' I asked. 'Then why'd you change your mind?'

She chuckled. 'You must really like me, Nick, or you wouldn't always be so disagreeable.'

I could not follow that line of reasoning. I said: 'Well, I'll see what Gilbert wants and run along.'

'I wish you could stay.'

'I'm sorry I can't,' I said again. 'Where'll I find him?'

'The second door to the – Will they really arrest Chris?'

'That depends,' I told her, 'on what kind of answers he gives them. He'll have to talk pretty straight to stay out.'

'Oh, he'll – ' she broke off, looked sharply at me, asked: 'You're not playing a trick on me? He's really that Rosewater?'

'The police are sure enough of it.'

'But the man who was here this afternoon didn't ask a single question about Chris,' she objected. 'He only asked me if I knew – '

'They weren't sure then,' I explained. 'It was just a half-idea.'

'But they're sure now?'

I nodded.

'How'd they find out?'

93

'From a girl he knows,' I said.

'Who?' Her eyes darkened a little, but her voice was under control.

'I can't remember her name.' Then I went back to the truth: 'The one that gave him his alibi for the afternoon of the murder.'

'Alibi?' she asked indignantly. 'Do you mean to tell me the police would take the word of a girl like that?'

'Like what?'

'You know what I mean.'

'I don't. Do you know the girl?'

'No,' she said as if I had insulted her. She narrowed her eyes and lowered her voice until it was not much more than a whisper: 'Nick, do you suppose he killed Julia?'

'What would he do that for?'

'Suppose he married me to get revenge on Clyde,' she said, 'and – You know he did urge me to come over here and try to get some money from Clyde. Maybe I suggested it – I don't know – but he did urge me. And then suppose he happened to run into Julia. She knew him, of course, because they worked for Clyde at the same time. And he knew I was going over to see her that afternoon and was afraid if I made her mad she might expose him to me and so – Couldn't that be?'

'That doesn't make any sense at all. Besides, you and he left here together that afternoon. He wouldn't've had time to – '

'But my taxicab was awfully slow,' she said, 'and then I may have stopped somewhere on – I think I did. I think I stopped at a drug store to get some aspirin.' She nodded energetically. 'I remember I did.'

'And he knew you were going to stop, because you had told him,' I suggested. 'You can't go on like this, Mimi. Murder's serious. It's nothing to frame people for just because they played tricks on you.'

'Tricks?' she asked, glaring at me. 'Why, that ...' She called Jorgensen all the usual profane, obscene, and otherwise insulting names, her voice gradually rising until towards the end she was screaming into my face.

When she stopped for breath I said: 'That's pretty cursing, but it – '

'He even had the nerve to hint that I might've killed her,' she told me. 'He didn't have nerve enough to ask me, but he kept leading up to it until I told him positively that – well, that I didn't do it.'

'That's not what you started to say. You told him positively what?'

She stamped her foot. 'Stop heckling me.'

'All right and to hell with you,' I said. 'Coming here wasn't my idea.' I started towards my hat and coat.

She ran after me, caught my arm. 'Please, Nick, I'm sorry. It's this rotten temper of mine. I don't know what I – '

Gilbert came in and said: 'I'll go along part of the way with you.'

Mimi scowled at him. 'You were listening.'

'How can I help it, the way you screamed?' he asked. 'Can I have some money?'

'And we haven't finished talking,' she said.

I looked at my watch. 'I've got to run, Mimi. It's late.'

'Will you come back after you get through with your date?'

'If it's not too late. Don't wait for me.'

'I'll be here,' she said. 'It doesn't matter how late it is.'

I said I would try to make it. She gave Gilbert his money. He and I went downstairs.

XIX

'I was listening,' Gilbert told me as we left the building. 'I think it's silly not to listen whenever you get a chance if you're interested in studying people, because they're never exactly the same as when you're with them. People don't like it when they know about it, of course, but' – he smiled – 'I don't suppose birds and animals like having naturalists spying on them either.'

'Hear much of it?' I asked.

'Oh, enough to know I didn't miss any of the important part.'

'And what'd you think of it?'

He pursed his lips, wrinkled his forehead, said judicially: 'It's hard to say exactly. Mamma's good at hiding things sometimes, but she's never much good at making them up. It's a funny thing – I suppose you've noticed it – the people who lie the most are nearly always the clumsiest at it, and they're easier to fool with lies than most people, too. You'd think they'd be on the look-out for lies, but they seem to be the very ones that will believe almost anything at all. I suppose you've noticed that, haven't you?'

'Yes.'

He said: 'What I wanted to tell you: Chris didn't come home last night. That's why Mamma's more upset than usual, and when I got the mail this morning there was a letter for him that I thought might have something in it, so I steamed it open.' He took a letter from his pocket and held it out to me. 'You'd better read it and then I'll seal it again and put it with tomorrow's mail in case he comes back, though I don't think he will.'

'Why don't you?' I asked as I took the letter.

'Well, he's really Rosewater. . . .'

'You say anything to him about it?'

'I didn't have a chance. I haven't seen him since you told me.'

I looked at the letter in my hand. The envelope was post-marked Boston, Massachusetts, December 27, 1932, and addressed in a slightly childish feminine hand to Mr Christian Jorgensen, Courtland Apts, New York, N.Y. 'How'd you happen to open it?' I asked, taking the letter out of the envelope.

'I don't believe in intuition,' he said, 'but there are prob-

96

ably odours, sounds, maybe something about the hand-writing, that you can't analyse, maybe aren't even conscious of, that influence you sometimes. I don't know what it was: I just felt there might be something important in it.'

'You often feel that way about the family mail?'

He glanced quickly at me as if to see whether I was spoofing, then said: 'Not often, but I have opened their mail before. I told you I was interested in studying people.'

I read the letter:

DEAR VIC –

Olga wrote me about you being back in the U.S. married to another woman and using the name of Christian Jorgensen. That is not right Vic as you very well know the same as leaving without word of any kind all these years. And no money. I know that you had to go away on account of that trouble you had with Mr Wynant but am sure he has long since forgot all about that and I do think you might have written to me as you know very well I have always been your friend and am willing to do anything within my power for you at any time. I do not want to scold you Vic but I have to see you. I will be off from the store Sunday and Monday on account of New Year and will come down to N.Y. Saturday night and must have a talk with you. Write me where you will meet me and what time as I do not want to make any trouble for you. Be sure and write me right away so I will get it in time.

Your true wife,
GEORGIA.

There was a street address.

I said: 'Well, well, well,' and put the letter back in its envelope. 'And you resisted the temptation to tell your mother about this?'

'Oh, I knew what her reaction would be. You saw how she carried on with just what you told her. What do you think I ought to do about it?'

'You ought to let me tell the police.'

He nodded immediately. 'If you think that's the best thing. You can show it to them if you want.'

I said: 'Thanks,' and put the letter in my pocket.

97

He said: 'Now there's another thing: I had some morphine I was experimenting with and somebody stole it, about twenty grains.'

'Experimenting how?'

'Taking it. I wanted to study the effects.'

'And how'd you like them?' I asked.

'Oh, I didn't expect to like it. I just wanted to know about it. I don't like things that dull my mind. That's why I don't often drink, or even smoke. I want to try cocaine, though, because that's supposed to sharpen the brain, isn't it?'

'It's supposed to. Who do you think copped the stuff?'

'I suspect Dorothy, because I have a theory about her. That's why I'm going over to Aunt Alice's for dinner: Dorry's still there and I want to find out. I can make her tell me anything.'

'Well, if she's been over there,' I asked, 'how could she –'

'She was home for a little while last night,' he said, 'and, besides, I don't know exactly when it was taken. Today was the first time I opened the box it was in for three or four days.'

'Did she know you had it?'

'Yes. That's one of the reasons I suspect her. I don't think anybody else did. I experimented on her too.'

'How'd she like it?'

'Oh, she liked it all right, but she'd have taken it anyhow. But what I want to ask you is could she have become an addict in a little time like that?'

'Like what?'

'A week – no – ten days.'

'Hardly, unless she thought herself into it. Did you give her much?'

'No.'

'Let me know if you find out,' I said, 'I'm going to grab a taxi here. Be seeing you.'

'You're coming over later tonight, aren't you?'

'If I can make it. Maybe I'll see you then.'

'Yes,' he said, 'and thanks awfully.'

At the first drug store I stopped to telephone Guild, not expecting to çatch him in his office, but hoping to learn how to reach him at his home. He was still there, though.

'Working late,' I said.

His 'That's what' sounded very cheerful.

I read Georgia's letter to him, gave him her address.

'Good pickings,' he said.

I told him Jorgensen had not been home since the day before.

'Think we'll find him in Boston?' he asked.

'Either there,' I guessed, 'or as far south as he could manage to get by this time.'

'We'll try 'em both,' he said, still cheerful. 'Now I got a bit of news for you. Our friend Nunheim was filled full of ·32s just about an hour after he copped the sneak on us – deader'n hell. The pills look like they come from the same gun that cut down the Wolf dame. The experts are matching 'em up now. I guess he wishes he'd stayed and talked to us.'

XX

NORA was eating a piece of cold duck with one hand and working on a jig-saw puzzle with the other when I got home.

'I thought you'd gone to live with her,' she said. 'You used to be a detective: find me a brownish piece shaped something like a snail with a long neck.'

'Piece of duck or puzzle? Don't let's go to the Edges' tonight: they're dull folk.'

'All right, but they'll be sore.'

'We wouldn't be that lucky,' I complained. 'They'd get sore at the Quinns and – '

'Harrison called you up. He told me to tell you now's the time to buy some McIntyre Porcupine – I think that's

99

right – to go with your Dome stock. He said it closed at twenty and a quarter.' She put a finger on her puzzle. 'The piece I want goes in there.'

I found the piece she wanted and told her, almost word for word, what had been done and said at Mimi's.

'I don't believe it,' she said. 'You made it up. There aren't any people like that. What's the matter with them? Are they the first of a new race of monsters?'

'I just tell you what happens; I don't explain it.'

'How would you explain it? There doesn't seem to be a single one in the family – now that Mimi's turned against her Chris – who has even the slightest reasonably friendly feeling for any of the others, and yet there's something very alike in all of them.'

'Maybe that explains it,' I suggested.

'I'd like to see Aunt Alice,' she said. 'Are you going to turn that letter over to the police?'

'I've already phoned Guild,' I replied, and told her about Nunheim.

'What does that mean?' she asked.

'For one thing, if Jorgensen's out of town, as I think he is, and the bullets are from the same gun that was used on Julia Wolf, and they probably are, then the police'll have to find his accomplice if they want to hang anything on him.'

'I'm sure if you were a good detective you'd be able to make it much clearer to me than it is.' She went to work on her puzzle again. 'Are you going back to see Mimi?'

'I doubt it. How about letting that dido rest while we get some dinner?'

The telephone rang and I said I would answer it. It was Dorothy Wynant. 'Hello. Nick?'

'The same. How are you, Dorothy?'

'Gil just got here and asked me about that you-know, and I wanted to tell you I did take it, but I only took it to try to keep him from becoming a dope-fiend.'

'What'd you do with it?' I asked.

'He made me give it back to him and he doesn't believe me, but, honestly, that's the only reason I took it.'

'I believe you.'

'Will you tell Gil, then? If you believe me, he will, because he thinks you know all about things like that.'

'I'll tell him as soon as I see him,' I promised.

There was a pause, then she asked: 'How's Nora?'

'Looks all right to me. Want to talk to her?'

'Well, yes, but there's something I want to ask you. Did – did Mamma say anything about me when you were over there today?'

'Not that I remember. Why?'

'And did Gil?'

'Only about the morphine.'

'Are you sure?'

'Pretty sure,' I said. 'Why?'

'It's nothing, really – if you're sure. It's just silly.'

'Right. I'll call Nora.' I went into the living-room. 'Dorothy wants to talk to you. Don't ask her to eat with us.'

When Nora returned from the telephone she had a look in her eye.

'Now what's up?' I asked.

'Nothing. Just "How are you" and all that.'

I said: 'If you're lying to the old man, God'll punish you.'

We went over to a Japanese place on Fifty-eighth Street for dinner and then I let Nora talk me into going to the Edges' after all.

Halsey Edge was a tall, scrawny man of fifty-something, with a pinched, yellow face and no hair at all. He called himself 'a ghoul by profession and inclination' – his only joke, if that is what it was – by which he meant he was an archaeologist, and he was very proud of his collection of battle-axes. He was not so bad once you had resigned yourself to the fact that you were in for occasional cataloguings of his armoury – stone axes, copper axes, bronze axes, double-bladed axes, faceted axes, polygonal axes, scalloped axes, hammer axes, adze axes, Mesopotamian axes, Hungarian axes, Nordic axes, and all of them looking pretty moth-eaten. It was his wife we objected to. Her name was Leda, but he called her Tip. She was very small and her hair, eyes, and skin, though naturally of different shades, were all muddy. She seldom sat – she perched on things – and liked to cock her head a little to one side. Nora had a theory that once when Edge opened an antique grave, Tip ran out of it, and Margot Innes always spoke of her as the gnome, pronouncing all the letters. She once told me that she did not think any literature of twenty years ago would live, because it had no psychiatry in it. They lived in a pleasant old three-storey house on the edge of Greenwich Village and their liquor was excellent.

A dozen or more people were there when we arrived. Tip introduced us to the ones we did not know and then backed me into a corner. 'Why didn't you tell me that those people I met at your place Christmas were mixed up in a murder mystery?' she asked, tilting her head to the left until her ear was practically resting on her shoulder.

'I don't know that they are. Besides, what's one murder mystery nowadays?'

She tilted her head to the right. 'You didn't even tell me you had taken the case.'

'I had done what? Oh, I see what you mean. Well, I hadn't and haven't. My getting shot ought to prove I was an innocent bystander.'

'Does it hurt much?'

'It itches. I forgot to have the dressing changed this afternoon.'

'Wasn't Nora utterly terrified?'

'So was I and so was the guy that shot me. There's Halsey. I haven't spoken to him yet.'

As I slid around her to escape she said: 'Harrison promised to bring the daughter tonight.'

I talked to Edge for a few minutes – chiefly about a place in Pennsylvania he was buying – then found myself a drink and listened to Larry Crowley and Phil Thames swap dirty stories until some woman came over and asked Phil – he taught at Columbia – one of the questions about technocracy that people were asking that week. Larry and I moved away.

We went over to where Nora was sitting. 'Watch yourself,' she told me. 'The gnome's hell-bent on getting the inside story of Julia Wolf's murder out of you.'

'Let her get it out of Dorothy,' I said. 'She's coming with Quinn.'

'I know.'

Larry said: 'He's nuts over that girl, isn't he? He told me he was going to divorce Alice and marry her.'

Nora said: 'Poor Alice,' sympathetically. She did not like Alice.

Larry said: 'That's according to how you look at it.' He liked Alice. 'I saw that fellow who's married to the girl's mother yesterday. You know, the tall fellow I met at your house.'

'Jorgensen.'

'That's it. He was coming out of a pawnshop on Sixth Avenue near Forty-sixth.'

'Talk to him?'

'I was in a taxi. It's probably polite to pretend you don't see people coming out of pawnshops, anyhow.'

Tip said: 'Sh-h-h,' in all directions, and Levi Oscant began to play the piano. Quinn and Dorothy arrived while he was playing. Quinn was drunk as a lord and Dorothy seemed to have something better than a glow.

She came over to me and whispered: 'I want to leave when you and Nora do.'

I said: 'You won't be here for breakfast.'

Tip said: 'Sh-h-h,' in my direction.

We listened to some more music.

Dorothy fidgeted beside me for a minute and whispered

again: 'Gil says you're going over to see Mamma later. Are you?'

'I doubt it.'

Quinn came unsteadily around to us. 'How're you, boy? How's you, Nora? Give him my message?' (Tip said: 'Sh-h-h,' at him. He paid no attention to her. Other people looked relieved and began to talk.) 'Listen, boy, you bank at the Golden Gate Trust in San Francisco, don't you?'

'Got a little money there.'

'Get it out, boy. I heard tonight they're plenty shaky.'

'All right. I haven't got much there, though.'

'No? What do you do with all your money?'

'Me and the French hoard gold.'

He shook his head solemnly. 'It's fellows like you that put the country on the bum.'

'And it's fellows like me that don't go on the bum with it,' I said. 'Where'd you get the skinful?'

'It's Alice. She's been sulking for a week. If I didn't drink I'd go crazy.'

'What's she sulking about?'

'About my drinking. She thinks – ' He leaned forward and lowered his voice confidentially. 'Listen. You're all my friends and I'm going to tell you what I'm going to do. I'm going to get a divorce and marry – '

He had tried to put an arm around Dorothy. She pushed it away and said: 'You're silly and you're tiresome. I wish you'd leave me alone.'

'She thinks I'm silly and tiresome,' he told me. 'You know why she don't want to marry me? I bet you don't. It's because she's in – '

'Shut up! Shut up, you drunken fool!' Dorothy began to beat his face with both hands. Her face was red, her voice shrill. 'If you say that again I'll kill you!'

I pulled Dorothy away from Quinn; Larry caught him, kept him from falling. He whimpered: 'She hit me, Nick.' Tears ran down his cheeks.

Dorothy had her face against my coat and seemed to be crying.

We had what audience there was. Tip came running, her face bright with curiosity. 'What is it, Nick?'

I said: 'Just a couple of playful drunks. They're all right. I'll see that they get home all right.'

Tip was not for that: she wanted them to stay at least until she had a chance to discover what had happened. She urged Dorothy to lie down awhile, offered to get something – whatever she meant by that – for Quinn, who was having trouble standing up now.

Nora and I took them out. Larry offered to go along, but we decided that was not necessary. Quinn slept in a corner of the taxicab during the ride to his apartment, and Dorothy sat stiff and silent in the other corner, with Nora between them. I clung to a folding seat and thought that anyway we had not stayed long at the Edges'.

Nora and Dorothy remained in the taxicab while I took Quinn upstairs. He was pretty limp.

Alice opened the door when I rang. She had on green pyjamas and held a hairbrush in one hand. She looked wearily at Quinn and spoke wearily: 'Bring it in.'

I took it in and spread it on a bed. It mumbled something I could not make out and moved one hand feebly back and forth, but its eyes stayed shut.

'I'll tuck him in,' I said, and loosened his tie.

Alice leaned on the foot of the bed. 'If you want to. I've given up doing it.'

I took off his coat, vest, and shirt.

'Where'd he pass out this time?' she asked with not much interest. She was still standing at the foot of the bed, brushing her hair now.

'The Edges'.' I unbuttoned his pants.

'With that little Wynant bitch?' The question was casual.

'There were a lot of people there.'

'Yes,' she said. 'He wouldn't pick a secluded spot.' She

brushed her hair a couple of times. 'So you don't think it's clubby to tell me anything.'

Her husband stirred a little and mumbled: 'Dorry.'

I took off his shoes.

Alice sighed. 'I can remember when he had muscles.' She stared at her husband until I took off the last of his clothes and rolled him under the covers. Then she sighed again and said: 'I'll get you a drink.'

'You'll have to make it short: Nora's waiting in the cab.'

She opened her mouth as if to speak, shut it, opened it again to say: 'Righto.'

I went into the kitchen with her.

Presently she said: 'It's none of my business, Nick, but what do people think of me?'

'You're like everybody else: some people like you, some people don't, and some have no feeling about it one way or the other.'

She frowned. 'That's not exactly what I meant. What do people think about my staying with Harrison with him chasing everything that's hot and hollow?'

'I don't know, Alice.'

'What do you think?'

'I think you probably know what you're doing and whatever you do is your own business.'

She looked at me with dissatisfaction. 'You'll never talk yourself into any trouble, will you?' She smiled bitterly. 'You know I'm only staying with him for his money, don't you? It may not be a lot to you, but it is to me – the way I was raised.'

'There's always divorce and alimony. You ought to have – '

'Drink your drink and get to hell out of here,' she said wearily.

XXI

NORA made a place for me between her and Dorothy in the taxicab. 'I want some coffee,' she said. 'Reuben's?'

I said: 'All right,' and gave the driver the address.

Dorothy asked timidly: 'Did his wife say anything?'

'She sent her love to you.'

Nora said: 'Stop being nasty.'

Dorothy said: 'I don't really like him, Nick. I won't ever see him again – honestly.' She seemed pretty sober now. 'It was – well, I was lonesome and he was somebody to run around with.'

I started to say something, but stopped when Nora poked me in the side.

Nora said: 'Don't worry about it. Harrison's always been a simpleton.'

'I don't want to stir things up,' I said, 'but I think he's really in love with the girl.'

Nora poked me in the side again.

Dorothy peered at my face in the dim light. 'You're – you're not – you're not making fun of me, Nick?'

'I ought to be.'

'I heard a new story about the gnome tonight,' Nora said in the manner of one who did not mean to be interrupted, and explained to Dorothy: 'That's Mrs Edge. Levi says. . . .' The story was funny enough if you knew Tip. Nora went on talking about her until we got out of the taxicab at Reuben's.

Herbert Macaulay was in the restaurant, sitting at a table with a plump, dark-haired girl in red. I waved at him and, after we had ordered some food, went over to speak to him.

'Nick Charles, Louise Jacobs,' he said. 'Sit down. What's news?'

'Jorgensen's Rosewater,' I told him.

'The hell he is!'

I nodded. 'And he seems to have a wife in Boston.'

'I'd like to see him,' he said slowly. 'I knew Rosewater. I'd like to make sure.'

'The police seem sure enough. I don't know whether they've found him yet. Think he killed Julia?'

Macaulay shook his head with emphasis. 'I can't see Rosewater killing anybody – not as I knew him – in spite of those threats he made. You remember I didn't take them very seriously at the time. What else has happened?' When I hesitated, he said: 'Louise is all right. You can talk.'

'It's not that. I've got to go back to my folks and food. I came over to ask if you'd got an answer to your ad. in this morning's *Times*.'

'Not yet. Sit down, Nick, there's a lot I want to ask you. You told the police about Wynant's letter, didn't – '

'Come up to lunch tomorrow and we'll bat it around. I've got to get back to my folks.'

'Who is the little blonde girl?' Louise Jacobs asked. 'I've seen her places with Harrison Quinn.'

'Dorothy Wynant.'

'You know Quinn?' Macaulay asked me.

'Ten minutes ago I was putting him to bed.'

Macaulay grinned. 'I hope you keep his acquaintance like that – social.'

'Meaning what?'

Macaulay's grin became rueful. 'He used to be my broker, and his advice led me right up to the poorhouse steps.'

'That's sweet,' I said. 'He's my broker now and I'm following his advice.'

Macaulay and the girl laughed. I pretended I was laughing and returned to my table.

Dorothy said: 'It's not midnight yet and Mamma said she'd be expecting you. Why don't we all go to see her?'

Nora was very carefully pouring coffee into her cup.

'What for?' I asked. 'What are you two up to now?'

It would have been hard to find two more innocent faces than theirs.

'Nothing, Nick,' Dorothy said. 'We thought it would be nice. It's early and – '

'And we all love Mimi.'

'No – o, but – '

'It's too early to go home,' Nora said.

'There are speakeasies,' I suggested, 'and night clubs and Harlem.'

Nora made a face. 'All your ideas are alike.'

'Want to go over to Barry's and try our luck at faro?'

Dorothy started to say yes, but stopped when Nora made another face.

'That's the way I feel about seeing Mimi again,' I said. 'I've had enough of her for one day.'

Nora sighed to show she was being patient. 'Well, if we're going to wind up in a speakeasy as usual, I'd rather go to your friend Studsy's, if you won't let him give us any more of that awful champagne. He's cute.'

'I'll do my best,' I promised and asked Dorothy: 'Did Gilbert tell you he caught Mimi and me in a compromising position?'

She tried to exchange glances with Nora, but Nora's glance was occupied with her plate. 'He – he didn't exactly say that.'

'Did he tell you about the letter?'

'From Chris's wife? Yes.' Her blue eyes glittered. 'Won't Mamma be furious!'

'You like it, though.'

'Suppose I do? What did she ever do to make me – '

Nora said: 'Nick, stop bullying the child.'

I stopped.

XXII

BUSINESS was good at the Pigiron Club. The place was full of people, noise, and smoke. Studsy came from behind the cash register to greet us. 'I was hoping you'd come in.' He shook my hand and Nora's and grinned broadly at Dorothy.

'Anything special?' I asked.

He made a bow. 'Everything's special with ladies like these.'

I introduced him to Dorothy.

He bowed to her and said something elaborate about any friend of Nick's and stopped a waiter. 'Pete, put a table up here for Mr Charles.'

'Pack them in like this every night?' I asked.

'I got no kick,' he said. 'They come once, they come back again. Maybe I ain't got no black marble cuspidors, but you don't have to spit out what you buy here. Want to lean against the bar whilst they're putting up the table?'

We said we did and ordered drinks.

'Hear about Nunheim?' I asked.

He looked at me for a moment before making up his mind to say: 'Uh-huh, I heard. His girl's down there' – he moved his head to indicate the other end of the room – 'celebrating, I guess.'

I looked past Studsy down the room and presently picked out big red-haired Miriam sitting at a table with half a dozen men and women. 'Hear who did it?' I asked.

'She says the police done it – he knew too much.'

'That's a laugh,' I said.

'That's a laugh,' he agreed. 'There's your table. Sit right down. I'll be back in a minute.'

We carried our glasses over to a table that had been squeezed in between two tables which had occupied a space large enough for one and made ourselves as nearly comfortable as we could.

Nora tasted her drink and shuddered. 'Do you suppose this could be the "bitter vetch" they used to put in crossword puzzles?'

Dorothy said: 'Oh, look.'

We looked and saw Shep Morelli coming towards us. His face had attracted Dorothy's attention. Where it was not dented it was swollen and its colouring ranged from deep purple around one eye to the pale pink of a piece of court-plaster on his chin.

He came to our table and leaned over a little to put both fists on it. 'Listen,' he said, 'Studsy says I ought to apologize.'

Nora murmured: 'Old Emily Post Studsy,' while I asked: 'Well?'

Morelli shook his battered head. 'I don't apologize for what I do – people've got to take it or leave it – but I don't mind telling you I'm sorry I lost my noddle and cracked down on you and I hope it ain't bothering you much and if there's anything I can do to square it I –'

'Forget it. Sit down and have a drink. This is Mr Morelli, Miss Wynant.'

Dorothy's eyes became wide and interested.

Morelli found a chair and sat down. 'I hope you won't hold it against me, neither,' he told Nora.

She said: 'It was fun.'

He looked at her suspiciously.

'Out on bail?' I asked.

'Uh-huh, this afternoon.' He felt his face gingerly with one hand. 'That's where the new ones come from. They had me resisting some more arrest just for good measure before they turned me loose.'

Nora said indignantly: 'That's horrible. You mean they really –'

I patted her hand.

Morelli said: 'You got to expect it.' His swollen lower lip moved in what was meant for a scornful smile. 'It's all right as long as it takes two or three of 'em to do it.'

Nora turned to me. 'Did you do things like that?'

'Who? Me?'

Studsy came over to us carrying a chair. 'They lifted his face, huh?' he said, nodding at Morelli. We made room for him and he sat down. He grinned complacently at Nora's drink and at Nora. 'I guess you don't get no better than that in your fancy Park Avenue joints – and you pay four bits a slug for it here.'

Nora's smile was weak, but it was a smile. She put her foot on mine under the table.

I asked Morelli: 'Did you know Julia Wolf in Cleveland?'

He looked sidewise at Studsy, who was leaning back in his chair, gazing around the room, watching his profits mount.

'When she was Rhoda Stewart,' I added.

He looked at Dorothy.

I said: 'You don't have to be cagey. She's Clyde Wynant's daughter.'

Studsy stopped gazing around the room and beamed on Dorothy. 'So you are? And how is your pappy?'

'But I haven't seen him since I was a little girl,' she said.

Morelli wet the end of a cigarette and put it between his swollen lips. 'I come from Cleveland.' He struck a match. His eyes were dull – he was trying to keep them dull. 'She wasn't Rhoda Stewart except once – Nancy Kane.' He looked at Dorothy again. 'Your father knows it.'

'Do you know my father?'

'We had some words once.'

'What about?' I asked.

'Her.' The match in his hand had burned down to his fingers. He dropped it, struck another, and lit his cigarette. He raised his eyebrows at me, wrinkling his forehead. 'Is this O.K.?'

'Sure. There's nobody here you can't talk in front of.'

'O.K. He was jealous as hell. I wanted to take a poke

112

at him, but she wouldn't let me. That was all right: he was her bank-roll.'

'How long ago was this?'

'Six months, eight months.'

'Have you seen him since she got knocked off?'

He shook his head. 'I never seen him but a couple of times, and this time I'm telling you about is the last.'

'Was she gypping him?'

'She don't say she is. I figure she is.'

'Why?'

'She's a wise head – plenty smart. She was getting dough somewheres. Once I wanted five grand.' He snapped his fingers. 'Cash.'

I decided against asking if he had paid her back. 'Maybe he gave it to her.'

'Sure – maybe.'

'Did you tell any of this to the police?' I asked.

He laughed once, contemptuously. 'They thought they could smack it out of me. Ask 'em what they think now. You're a right guy, I don't – ' He broke off, took the cigarette from between his lips. 'The earysipelas kid,' he said, and put out a hand to touch the ear of a man who, sitting at one of the tables we had squeezed in between, had been leaning further and further back towards us.

The man jumped and turned a startled, pale, pinched face around over his shoulder at Morelli.

Morelli said: 'Pull in that lug – it's getting in our drinks.'

The man stammered: 'I d-didn't mean nothing, Shep,' and rammed his belly into his table trying to get as far as possible from us, which still did not take him out of earshot.

Morelli said: 'You won't ever mean nothing, but that don't keep you from trying,' and returned his attention to me. 'I'm willing to go all the way with you – the kid's dead, it's not going to hurt her any – but Mulrooney ain't got a wrecking crew that can get it out of me.'

'Swell,' I said. 'Tell me about her, where you first ran

113

into her, what she did before she tied up with Wynant where he found her.'

'I ought to have a drink.' He twisted himself around in his chair and called: 'Hey, garsong – you with the boy on your back!'

The somewhat hunchbacked waiter Studsy had called Pete pushed through people to our table and grinned affectionately down at Morelli. 'What'll it be?' He sucked a tooth noisily.

We gave our orders and the waiter went away.

Morelli said: 'Me and Nancy lived in the same block. Old man Kane had a candy store on the corner. She used to pinch cigarettes for me.' He laughed. 'Her old man kicked hell out of me once for showing her how to get nickels out of the telephone with a piece of wire. You know, the old style ones. We couldn't've been more than in the third grade.' He laughed again, low in his throat. 'I wanted to glaum some fixtures from a row of houses they were building around the corner and plant 'em in his cellar and tell Schultz, the cop on the beat, to pay him back, but she wouldn't let me.'

Nora said: 'You must've been a little darling.'

'I was that,' he said fondly. 'Listen. Once when I was no more'n five or – '

A feminine voice said: 'I thought that was you.'

I looked up and saw it was red-haired Miriam speaking to me. I said: 'Hello.'

She put her hands on her hips and stared sombrely at me. 'So he knew too much for you.'

'Maybe, but he took it on the lam down the fire-escape with his shoes in his hand before he told us any of it.'

'Boloney!'

'All right. What do you think he knew that was too much for us?'

'Where Wynant is,' she said.

'So? Where is he?'

'I don't know. Art knew.'

'I wish he'd told us. We – '

'Boloney!' she said again. 'You know and the police know. Who do you think you're kidding?'

'I'm not kidding. I don't know where Wynant is.'

'You're working for him and the police are working with you. Don't kid me. Art thought knowing was going to get him a lot of money, poor sap. He didn't know what it was going to get him.'

'Did he tell you he knew?' I asked.

'I'm not as dumb as you think. He told me he knew something that was going to get him big dough and I've seen how it worked out. I guess I can put two and two together.'

'Sometimes the answer's four,' I said, 'and sometimes it's twenty-two. I'm not working for Wynant. Now don't say "Boloney" again. Do you want to help – '

'No. He was a rat and he held out on the people he was ratting for. He asked for what he got, only don't expect me to forget that I left him with you and Guild, and the next time anybody saw him he was dead.'

'I don't want you to forget anything. I'd like you to remember whether – '

'I've got to go,' she said, and walked away. Her carriage was remarkably graceful.

'I don't know as I'd want to be mixed up with that dame,' Studsy said thoughtfully. 'She's mean medicine.'

Morelli winked at me.

Dorothy touched my arm. 'I don't understand, Nick.'

I told her that was all right and addressed Morelli: 'You were telling us about Julia Wolf.'

'Uh-huh. Well, old man Kane booted her out when she was fifteen or sixteen and got in some kind of jam with a high-school teacher and she took up with a guy called Face Peppler, a smart kid if he didn't talk too much. I remember once me and Face were – ' He broke off and cleared his throat. 'Anyways, Face and her stuck together – what the hell – it must be five, six years, throwing out the

115

time he was in the army and she was living with some guy that I can't remember his name – a cousin of Dick O'Brien's, a skinny, dark-headed guy that liked his liquor. But she went back to Face when he come out of the army, and they stuck together till they got nailed trying to shake down some bird from Toronto. Face took it and got her off with six months – they gave him the business. Last I heard he was still in. I saw her when she came out – she touched me for a couple hundred to blow town. I hear from her once, when she sends it back to me and tells me Julia Wolf's her name now and she likes the big city fine, but I know Face is hearing from her right along. So when I move here in '28, I look her up. She's – '

Miriam came back and stood with her hands on her hips as before. 'I've been thinking over what you said. You must think I'm pretty dumb.'

'No,' I said, not very truthfully.

'It's a cinch I'm not dumb enough to fall for that song and dance you tried to give me. I can see things when they're right in front of me.'

'All right.'

'It's not all right. You killed Art and – '

'Not so loud, girlie.' Studsy rose and took her arm. His voice was soothing. 'Come along. I want to talk to you.' He led her towards the bar.

Morelli winked again. 'He likes that. Well, I was saying I looked her up when I moved here, and she told me she had this job with Wynant and he was nuts about her and she was sitting pretty. It seems they learned her shorthand in Ohio when she was doing her six months and she figures maybe it'll be an in to something – you know, maybe she can get a job somewheres where they'll go out and leave the safe open. An agency had sent her over to do a couple days' work for Wynant and she figured maybe he'd be worth more for a long pull than for a quick tap and a getaway, so she give him the business and wound up with a steady connexion. She was smart enough to tell him she had a record and was trying to go straight now and all that, so's not to have the racket spoiled if he found out anyhow, because she said his lawyer was a little leery of her and might have her looked up. I don't know just what she was doing, you understand, because it's her game and she don't need my help, and even if we are pals in a way, there's no sense in telling me anything I might want to go to her boss with. Understand, she wasn't my girl or anything – we was just a couple of old friends, been kids playing together. Well, I used to see her every once in a while – we used to come here a lot – till he kicked up too much of a fuss and then she said she was going to cut it out, she wasn't going to lose a soft bed over a few drinks with me. So that was that. That was October, I guess, and she stuck to it. I haven't seen her since.'

'Who else did she run around with?' I asked.

Morelli shook his head. 'I don't know. She don't do much talking about people.'

'She was wearing a diamond engagement ring. Know anything about it?'

'Nothing except she didn't get it from me. She wasn't wearing it when I see her.'

'Do you think she meant to throw in with Peppler again when he got out?'

'Maybe. She didn't seem to worry much about him being in, but she liked to work with him all right and I guess they'd've teamed up again.'

'And how about the cousin of Dick O'Brien, the skinny, dark-headed lush? What became of him?'

Morelli looked at me in surprise. 'Search me.'

Studsy returned alone. 'Maybe I'm wrong,' he said as he sat down, 'but I think somebody could do something with that cluck if they took hold of her right.'

Morelli said: 'By the throat.'

Studsy grinned good-naturedly. 'No. She's trying to get somewhere. She works hard at her singing lessons and – '

Morelli looked at his empty glass and said: 'This tiger milk of yours must be doing her pipes a lot of good.' He turned his head to yell at Pete: 'Hey, you with the knapsack, some more of the same. We got to sing in the choir tomorrow.'

Pete said: 'Coming up, Sheppy.' His lined, grey face lost its dull apathy when Morelli spoke to him.

An immensely fat blond man – so blond he was nearly albino – who had been sitting at Miriam's table came over and said to me in a thin, tremulous, effeminate voice: 'So you're the party who put it to little Art Nunhei – '

Morelli hit the fat man in his fat belly, as hard as he could without getting up. Studsy, suddenly on his feet, leaned over Morelli and smashed a big fist into the fat man's face. I noticed, foolishly, that he still led with his right. Hunchbacked Pete came up behind the fat man and banged his empty tray down with full force on the fat man's head. The fat man fell back, upsetting three people and a table. Both bar-tenders were with us by then. One of them hit the fat man with a blackjack as he tried to get up, knocking him forward on hands and knees, the other put a hand down inside the fat man's collar in back, twisting the collar to choke him. With Morelli's help they got the fat man to his feet and hustled him out.

Pete looked after them and sucked a tooth. 'That goddamned Sparrow,' he exclaimed to me, 'you can't take no chances on him when he's drinking.'

Studsy was at the next table, the one that had been upset, helping people pick up themselves and their possessions. 'That's bad,' he was saying, 'bad for business, but where are you going to draw the line? I ain't running a dive, but I ain't trying to run a young ladies' seminary neither.'

Dorothy was pale, frightened; Nora wide-eyed and amazed. 'It's a madhouse,' she said. 'What'd they do that for?'

'You know as much about it as I do,' I told her.

Morelli and the bar-tenders came in again, looking pretty pleased with themselves. Morelli and Studsy returned to their seats at our table.

'You boys are impulsive,' I said.

Studsy repeated: 'Impulsive,' and laughed: 'Ha-ha-ha.'

Morelli was serious. 'Any time that guy starts anything, you got to start it first. It's too late when he gets going. We seen him like that before, ain't we, Studsy?'

'Like what?' I asked. 'He hadn't done anything.'

'He hadn't, all right,' Morelli said slowly, 'but it's a kind of feeling you get about him sometimes. Ain't that right, Studsy?'

Studsy said: 'Uh-huh, he's hysterical.'

XXIII

IT was about two o'clock when we said good-night to Studsy and Morelli and left the Pigiron Club.

Dorothy slumped down in her corner of the taxicab and said: 'I'm going to be sick. I know I am.' She sounded as if she was telling the truth.

Nora said: 'That booze.' She put her head on my shoulder. 'Your wife is drunk, Nicky. Listen, you've got to tell me what happened – everything. Not now, tomorrow. I don't understand a thing that was said or a thing that was done. They're marvellous.'

Dorothy said: 'Listen, I can't go to Aunt Alice's like this. She'd have a fit.'

Nora said: 'They oughtn't've hit that fat man like that, though it must've been funny in a cruel way.'

Dorothy said: 'I suppose I'd better go to Mamma's.'

Nora said: 'Erysipelas hasn't got anything to do with ears. What's a lug, Nicky?'

'An ear.'

Dorothy said: 'Aunt Alice would have to see me because I forgot the key and I'd have to wake her up.'

Nora said: 'I love you, Nicky, because you smell nice and know such fascinating people.'

Dorothy said: 'It's not much out of your way to drop me at Mamma's, is it?'

I said: 'No,' and gave the driver Mimi's address.

Nora said: 'Come home with us.'

Dorothy said: 'No – o, I'd better not.'

Nora asked: 'Why not?' and Dorothy said: 'Well, I don't think I ought to,' and that kind of thing went on until the taxicab stopped at the Courtland.

I got out and helped Dorothy out. She leaned heavily on my arm. 'Please come up, just for a minute.'

Nora said: 'Just for a minute,' and got out of the taxicab.

I told the driver to wait. We went upstairs. Dorothy rang the bell, Gilbert, in pyjamas and bathrobe, opened the door. He raised one hand in a warning gesture and said in a low voice: 'The police are here.'

Mimi's voice came from the living-room: 'Who is it, Gil?'

'Mr and Mrs Charles and Dorothy.'

Mimi came to meet us as we went in. 'I never was so glad to see anybody. I just didn't know which way to turn.' She had on a pinkish satin robe over a pinkish silk night-gown, and her face was pink and by no means unhappy. She ignored Dorothy, squeezed one of Nora's hands, one of mine. 'Now I'm going to stop worrying and leave it all up to you, Nick. You'll have to tell the foolish little woman what to do.'

Dorothy, behind me, said: 'Boloney!' under her breath, but with a lot of feeling.

Mimi did not show that she had heard her daughter. Still holding our hands, she drew us back towards the living-room, chattering: 'You know Lieutenant Guild. He's been very nice, but I'm sure I must have tried his patience. I've been so – well – I mean I've been so bewildered. But now you're here and – '

We went into the living-room.

Guild said, 'Hello,' to me and, 'Good evening, ma'am,' to Nora. The man with him, the one he had called Andy and who had helped him search our rooms the morning of Morelli's visit, nodded and grunted at us.

'What's up?' I asked.

Guild looked at Mimi out of the corners of his eyes, then at me, and said: 'The Boston police found Jorgensen or Rosewater or whatever you want to call him at his first wife's place and asked him some questions for us. The chief answer seems to be he don't have anything to do with Julia Wolf getting killed or not getting killed and Mrs Jorgensen can prove it because she's been holding out what amounts to the goods on Wynant.' His eyes slid sidewise in their sockets to focus on Mimi again. 'The lady kind of don't want to say yes and kind of don't want to say no. To tell you the truth, Mr Charles, I don't know what to make of her in a lot of ways.'

I could understand that. I said: 'She's probably frightened,' and Mimi tried to look frightened. 'Has he been divorced from the first wife?'

'Not according to the first wife.'

Mimi said: 'She's lying, I bet.'

I said: 'Sh-h-h. Is coming back to New York?'

'It looks like he's going to make us extradite him if we want him. Boston says he's squawking his head off for a lawyer.'

'Do you want him that bad?'

Guild moved his big shoulders. 'If bringing him back'll help us on this murder. I don't care much about any of the old charges of the bigamy. I never believe in hounding a man over things that are none of my business.'

I asked Mimi: 'Well?'

'Can I talk to you alone?'

I looked at Guild, who said: 'Anything that'll help.'

Dorothy touched my arm. 'Nick, listen to me first. I – ' She broke off. Everybody was staring at her.

'What?' I asked.

'I – I want talk to you first.'

'Go ahead.'

'I mean alone,' she said.

I patted her hand. 'Afterwards.'

Mimi led me into her bedroom and carefully shut the door. I sat on the bed and lit a cigarette. Mimi leaned back against the door and smiled at me very gently and trustingly. Half a minute passed that way.

Then she said, 'You do like me, Nick,' and when I said nothing she asked: 'Don't you?'

'No.'

She laughed and came away from the door. 'You mean you don't approve of me.' She sat on the bed beside me. 'But you do like me well enough to help me?'

'That depends.'

'Depends on wha – '

The door opened and Dorothy came in. 'Nick, I've got to – '

Mimi jumped up and confronted her daughter. 'Get out of here,' she said through her teeth.

Dorothy flinched, but she said: 'I won't. You're not going to make a – '

Mimi slashed Dorothy across the mouth with the back of her right hand. 'Get out of here.'

Dorothy screamed and put a hand to her mouth. Holding it there, holding her wide frightened eyes on Mimi's face, she backed out of the room.

Mimi shut the door again.

I said: 'You must come over to our place some time and bring your little white whips.'

She did not seem to hear me. Her eyes were heavy, brooding, and her lips were thrust out a little in a half-smile, and when she spoke, her voice seemed heavier, throatier, than usual. 'My daughter's in love with you.'

'Nonsense.'

'She is and she's jealous of me. She has absolute spasms whenever I get within ten feet of you.' She spoke as if thinking of something else.

'Nonsense. Maybe she's got a little hang-over from that crush she had on me when she was twelve, but that's all it is.'

Mimi shook her head. 'You're wrong, but never mind.' She sat down on the bed beside me again. 'You've got to help me out of this. I – '

'Sure,' I said. 'You're a delicate *fleur* that needs a great big man's protection.'

'Oh, that?' She waved a hand at the door through which Dorothy had gone. 'You're surely not getting – Why, it's nothing you haven't heard about before – and seen and done, for that matter. It's nothing to worry you.' She smiled as before, with heavy, brooding eyes, and lips thrust out a little. 'If you want Dorry, take her, but don't get sentimental about it. But never mind that. Of course I'm not a delicate *fleur*. You never thought I was.'

'No,' I agreed.

'Well, then,' she said with an air of finality.

'Well then what?'

'Stop being so damned coquettish,' she said. 'You know what I mean. You understand me as well as I understand you.'

'Just about, but you've been doing the coquetting ever since – '

'I know. That was a game. I'm not playing now. That guy made a fool of me, Nick, an out and out fool, and now he's in trouble and expects me to help him. I'll help him.' She put a hand on my knee and her pointed nails dug into my flesh. 'The police, they don't believe me. How can I make them believe that he's lying, that I know nothing more than I've told them about the murder?'

'You probably can't,' I said slowly, 'especially since Jorgensen's only repeating what you told me a few hours ago.'

She caught her breath, and her nails dug into me again. 'Did you tell them that?'

'Not yet.' I took her hand off my knee.

She sighed with relief. 'And of course you won't tell them now, will you?'

'Why not?'

'Because it's a lie. He lied and I lied. I didn't find anything, anything at all.'

I said: 'We're back where we were earlier, and I believe you just as much now as I did then. What happened to those new terms we were on? You understanding me, me understanding you, no coquetting, no games, no playing.'

She slapped my hand lightly. 'All right. I did find something – not much, but something – and I'm not going to give it up to help that guy. You can understand how I feel about it, Nick. You'd feel the same –'

'Maybe,' I said, 'but the way it stands, I've got no reason for putting in with you. Your Chris is no enemy of mine. I've got nothing to gain by helping you frame him.'

She sighed. 'I've been thinking about that a lot. I don't suppose what money I could give you would mean much to you now' – she smiled crookedly – 'nor my beautiful white body. But aren't you interested in saving Clyde?'

'Not necessarily.'

She laughed at that. 'I don't know what that means.'

'It might mean I don't think he needs saving. The police haven't got much on him. He's screwy, he was in town the day Julia was killed, and she had been gypping him. That's not enough to arrest him on.'

She laughed again. 'But with my contribution?'

'I don't know. What is it?' I asked, and went on without waiting for the answer I did not expect. 'Whatever it is, you're being a sap, Mimi. You've got Chris cold on bigamy. Sock that to him. There's no –'

She smiled sweetly and said: 'But I am holding that in reserve to use after this if he –'

'If he gets past the murder charge, huh? Well, it won't work out that way, lady. You can get him about three days in jail. By that time the District Attorney will have questioned him and checked up on him enough to know that he didn't kill Julia and that you've been making a chump of the D.A., and when you spring your little bigamy charge the D.A. will tell you to go jump in the lake, and he'll refuse to prosecute.'

'But he can't do that, Nick.'

'Can and will,' I assured her, 'and if he can dig up proof that you're holding out something he'll make it as tough for you as he can.'

She chewed her lower lip, asked: 'You're being honest with me?'

'I'm telling you exactly what'll happen, unless district attorneys have changed a lot since my day.'

She chewed her lip some more. 'I don't want him to get off,' she said presently, 'and I don't want to get into any trouble myself.' She looked up at me. 'If you're lying to me, Nick . . .'

'There's nothing you can do about it except believe me or disbelieve me.'

She smiled and put a hand on my cheek and kissed me on the mouth and stood up. 'Well, I'm going to believe you.' She walked down to the other end of the room and back again. Her eyes were shiny, her face pleasantly excited.

'I'll call Guild,' I said.

'No, wait. I'd rather see what you think of it first.'

'All right, but no clowning.'

'You're certainly afraid of your shadow,' she said, 'but don't worry, I'm not going to play any tricks on you.'

I said that would be swell and how about showing me whatever she had to show me. 'The others will be getting restless.'

She went around the bed to a closet, opened the door, pushed some clothes aside, and put a hand among other clothes behind them. 'That's funny,' she said.

'Funny?' I stood up. 'It's a panic. It'll have Guild rolling on the floor.' I started towards the door.

'Don't be so bad-tempered,' she said. 'I've got it.' She turned to me holding a wadded handkerchief in her hand. As I approached, she opened the handkerchief to show me a three-inch length of watch-chain, broken at one end, attached at the other to a small gold knife. The handkerchief was a woman's and there were brown stains on it.

'Well?' I asked.,

'It was in her hand and I saw it when they left me with her and I knew it was Clyde's, so I took it.'

'You're sure it's his?'

'Yes,' she said impatiently. 'See, they're gold, silver, and copper links. He had it made out of the first batches of metal that came through that smelting process he invented. Anybody who knows him at all well can identify it – there can't be another like it.' She turned the knife over to let me see the C M W engraved in it. 'They're his initials. I never saw the knife before, but I'd know the chain anywhere. Clyde's worn it for years.'

'Did you remember it well enough that you could've described it without seeing it again?'

'Of course.'

'Is that your handkerchief?'

'Yes.'

'And the stain on it's blood?'

'Yes. The chain was in her hand – I told you – and there was some blood on them.' She frowned at me. 'Don't you – You act as if you don't believe me.'

'Not exactly,' I said, 'but I think you ought to be sure you're telling your story straight this time.'

She stamped her foot. 'You're –' She laughed and anger went out of her face. 'You can be the most annoying man. I'm telling the truth now, Nick. I've told you everything that happened exactly as it happened.'

'I hope so. It's about time. You're sure Julia didn't come to enough to say anything while you were alone with her?'

'You're trying to make me mad again. Of course I'm sure.'

'All right,' I said. 'Wait here. I'll get Guild, but if you tell him the chain was in Julia's hand and she wasn't dead yet, he's going to wonder whether you didn't have to rough her up a little to get it away from her.'

She opened her eyes wide. 'What should I tell him?'

I went out and shut the door.

XXIV

NORA, looking a little sleepy, was entertaining Guild and Andy in the living-room. The Wynant offspring were not in sight.

'Go ahead,' I told Guild. 'First door to the left. I think she's readied up for you.'

'Crack her?' he asked.

I nodded.

'What'd you get?'

'See what you get and we'll put them together and see how they add up,' I suggested.

'O.K. Come on, Andy.' They went out.

'Where's Dorothy?' I asked.

Nora yawned. 'I thought she was with you and her mother. Gilbert's around somewhere. He was here till a few minutes ago. Do we have to hang around long?'

'Not long.' I went back down the passage-way past Mimi's door to another bedroom door, which was open, and looked in. Nobody was there. A door facing it was shut. I knocked on it.

Dorothy's voice: 'What is it?'

'Nick,' I said and went in.

She was lying on her side on a bed, dressed except for her slippers. Gilbert was sitting on the bed beside her. Her mouth seemed a little puffy, but it may have been from

127

crying: her eyes were red. She raised her head to stare sullenly at me.

'Still want to talk to me?' I asked.

Gilbert got up from the bed. 'Where's Mamma?'

'Talking to the police.'

He said something I did not catch and left the room.

Dorothy shuddered. 'He gives me the creeps,' she said, and then remembered to stare sullenly at me again.

'Still want to talk to me?'

'What made you turn against me like that?'

'You're being silly.' I sat down where Gilbert had been sitting. 'Do you know anything about this knife and chain your mother's supposed to have found?'

'No. Where?'

'What'd you want to tell me?'

'Nothing – now,' she said disagreeably, 'except you might at least wipe her lipstick off your mouth.'

I wiped it off. She snatched the handkerchief from my hand and rolled over to pick up a package of matches from the table on that side of the bed. She struck a match.

'That's going to stink like hell,' I said.

She said: 'I don't care,' but she blew out the match. I took the handkerchief, went to the window, opened it, dropped the handkerchief out, shut the window, and went back to my seat on the bed. 'If that makes you feel any better.'

'What did Mamma say – about me?'

'She said you're in love with me.'

She sat up abruptly. 'What did you say?'

'I said you just liked me from when you were a kid.'

Her lower lip twitched. 'Do – do you think that's what it is?'

'What else could it be?'

'I don't know.' She began to cry. 'Everybody's made so much fun of me about it – Mamma and Gilbert and Harrison – I – '

I put my arms around her. 'To hell with them.'

After a while she asked: 'Is Mamma in love with you?'

'Good God, no! She hates men more than any woman I've ever known.'

'But she's always having some sort of – '

'That's the body. Don't let it fool you. Mimi hates men – all of us – bitterly.'

She had stopped crying. She wrinkled her forehead and said: 'I don't understand. Do you hate her?'

'Not as a rule.'

'Now?'

'I don't think so. She's being stupid and she's sure she's being very clever, and that's a nuisance, but I don't think I hate her.'

'I do,' Dorothy said.

'So you told me last week. Something I meant to ask you: did you know or did you ever see the Arthur Nunheim we were talking about in the speakeasy tonight?'

She looked sharply at me. 'You're just trying to change the subject.'

'I want to know. Did you?'

'No.'

'He was mentioned in the newspapers,' I reminded her. 'He was the one who told the police about Morelli knowing Julia Wolf.'

'I didn't remember his name,' she said. 'I don't remember ever having heard it until tonight.'

I described him. 'Ever seen him?'

'No.'

'He may have been known as Albert Norman sometimes. Does that sound familiar?'

'No.'

'Know any of the people we saw at Studsy's tonight? Or anything about them?'

'No. Honestly, Nick, I'd tell you if I knew anything at all that might help you.'

'No matter who it hurt?'

'Yes,' she said immediately, then: 'What do you mean?'

'You know damned well what I mean.'

She put her hands over her face, and her words were barely audible: 'I'm afraid, Nick. I – ' She jerked her hands down as someone knocked on the door.

'All right,' I called.

Andy opened the door far enough to stick his head in. He tried to keep curiosity from showing in his face while saying: 'The Lieutenant wants to see you.'

'Be right out,' I promised.

He opened the door wider. 'He's waiting.' He gave me what was probably meant to be a significant wink, but a corner of his mouth moved more than his eye did and the result was a fairly startling face.

'I'll be back,' I told Dorothy, and followed him out.

He shut the door behind me and put his mouth close to my ear. 'The kid was at the keyhole,' he muttered.

'Gilbert?'

'Yep. He had time to get away from it when he heard me coming, but he was there, right enough.'

'That's mild for him,' I said. 'How'd you all make out with Mrs J.?'

He pucked his thick lips up in an *o* and blew breath out noisily. 'What a dame!'

XXV

WE went into Mimi's bedroom. She was sitting in a deep chair by a window looking very pleased with herself. She smiled gaily at me and said: 'My soul is spotless now. I've confessed everything.'

Guild stood by a table wiping his face with a handkerchief. There were still some drops of sweat on his temples, and his face seemed old and tired. The knife and chain, and the handkerchief they had been wrapped in, were on the table.

'Finished?' I asked.

'I don't know, and that's a fact,' he said. He turned his head to address Mimi: 'Would you say we were finished?'

Mimi laughed. 'I can't imagine what more there would be.'

'Well,' Guild said slowly, somewhat reluctantly, 'in that case I guess I'd like to talk to Mr Charles, if you'll excuse us for a couple of minutes.' He folded his handkerchief carefully and put it in his pocket.

'You can talk here.' She got up from the chair. 'I'll go out and talk to Mrs Charles till you're through.' She tapped my cheek playfully with the tip of a forefinger as she passed me. 'Don't let them say too horrid things about me, Nicky.'

Andy opened the door for her, shut it behind her, and made the *o* and the blowing noise again.

I lay down on the bed. 'Well,' I asked, 'what's what?'

Guild cleared his throat. 'She told us about finding this here chain and knife on the floor where the Wolf dame had most likely broke it off fighting with Wynant, and she told us the reasons why she's hid it till now. Between me and you, that don't make any too much sense, looking at it reasonably, but maybe that ain't the way to look at it in this case. To tell you the plain truth, I don't know what to make of her in a lot of ways, I don't for a fact.'

'The chief thing,' I advised them, 'is not to let her tire you out. When you catch her in a lie, she admits it and gives you another lie to take its place and, when you catch her in that one, admits it and gives you still another, and so on. Most people – even women – get discouraged after you've caught them in the third or fourth straight lie and fall back on either the truth or silence, but not Mimi. She keeps trying and you've got to be careful or you'll find yourself believing her, not because she seems to be telling the truth, but simply because you're tired of disbelieving her.'

Guild said: 'Hm-m-m. Maybe.' He put a finger inside his collar. He seemed very uncomfortable. 'Look here, do you think she killed that dame?'

I discovered that Andy was staring at me so intently that his eyes bulged. I sat up and put my feet on the floor. 'I wish I knew. That chain business looks like a plant all right, but. ... We can find out whether he had a chain like that, maybe whether he still has it. If she remembered the chain as well as she said she did, there's no reason why she couldn't have told a jeweller how to make one, and anybody can buy a knife and have any initials they want engraved on it. There's plenty to be said against the probability of her having gone that far. If she did plant it, it's more likely she had the original chain – maybe she's had it for years – but all that's something for you folks to check up.'

'We're doing the best we can,' Guild said patiently. 'So you do think she did it?'

'The murder?' I shook my head. 'I haven't got that far yet. How about Nunheim? Did the bullets match up?'

'They did – from the same gun as was used on the dame – all five of them.'

'He was shot five times?'

'He was, and close enough to burn his clothes.'

'I saw his girl, the big red-head, tonight in a speak,' I told him. 'She's saying you and I killed him because he knew too much.'

He said: 'Hm-m-m. What speak was that? I might want to talk to her.'

'Studsy Burke's Pigiron Club,' I said, and gave him the address. 'Morelli hangs out there, too. He tells me Julia Wolf's real name is Nancy Kane and she has a boy friend doing time in Ohio – Face Peppler.'

From the tone of Guild's 'Yes?' I imagined he had already found out about Peppler and about Julia's past. 'And what else did you pick up in your travels?'

'A friend of mine – Larry Crowley, a press agent – saw Jorgensen coming out of a hock-shop on Sixth near Forty-sixth yesterday afternoon.'

'Yes?'

'You don't seem to get excited about my news. I'm – '

Mimi opened the door and came in with glasses, whisky, and mineral water on a tray. 'I thought you'd like a drink,' she said cheerfully.

We thanked her.

She put the tray on the table, said: 'I don't mean to interrupt,' smiled at us with that air of amused tolerance which women like to affect towards male gatherings, and went out.

'You were saying something,' Guild reminded me.

'Just that if you people think I'm not coming clean with you, you ought to say so. We've been playing along together so far and I wouldn't want – '

'No, no,' Guild said hastily, 'it's nothing like that, Mr Charles.' His face had reddened a little. 'I been – The fact is the Commissioner's been riding us for action and I guess I been kind of passing it on. This second murder's made things tough.' He turned to the tray on the table. 'How'll you have yours?'

'Straight, thanks. No leads on it?'

'Well, the same gun and a lot of bullets, same as with her, but that's about all. It was a rooming-house hallway in between a couple stores. Nobody there claims they know Nunheim or Wynant or anybody else we can connect. The door's left unlocked, anybody could walk in, but that don't make too much sense when you come to think of it.'

'Nobody saw or heard anything?'

'Sure, they heard the shooting, but they didn't see anybody doing it.' He gave me a glass of whisky.

'Find any empty shells?' I asked.

He shook his head. 'Neither time. Probably a revolver.'

'And he emptied it both times – counting the shot that hit her telephone – if, like a lot of people, he carried an empty chamber under the hammer.'

Guild lowered the glass he was raising towards his mouth. 'You're not trying to find a Chinese angle on it, are you?' he complained. 'Just because they shoot like that.'

'No, but any kind of angle would help some. Find out where Nunheim was the afternoon the girl was killed?'

'Uh-huh. Hanging around the girl's building – part of the time anyhow. He was seen in front and he was seen in back, if you're going to believe people that didn't think much of it at the time and haven't got any reason for lying about it. And the day before the killing he had been up to her apartment, according to an elevator boy. The boy says he came down right away and he don't know whether he got in or not.'

I said: 'So. Maybe Miriam's right, maybe he did know too much. Find out anything about the four thousand difference between what Macaulay gave her and what Clyde Wynant says he got from her?'

'No.'

'Morelli says she always had plenty of money. He says she once lent him five thousand in cash.'

Guild raised his eyebrows. 'Yes?'

'Yes. He also says Wynant knew about her record.'

'Seems to me,' Guild said slowly, 'Morelli did a lot of talking to you.'

'He likes to talk. Find out anything more about what Wynant was working on when he left, or what he was going away to work on?'

'No. You're kind of interested in that shop of his.'

'Why not? He's an inventor, the shop's his place. I'd like to to have a look at it some time.'

'Help yourself. Tell me some more about Morelli, and how you go about getting him to open up.'

'He likes to talk. Do you know a fellow called Sparrow? A big, fat, pale fellow with a pansy voice?'

Guild frowned. 'No. Why?'

'He was there – with Miriam – and wanted to take a crack at me, but they wouldn't let him.'

'And what'd he want to do that for?'

'I don't know. Maybe because she told him I helped knock Nunheim off – helped you.'

Guild said: 'Oh.' He scratched his chin with a thumbnail, looked at his watch. 'It's getting kind of late. Suppose you drop in and see me some time tomorrow – today.'

I said: 'Sure,' instead of the things I was thinking, nodded at him and Andy, and went out to the living-room.

Nora was sleeping on the sofa. Mimi put down the book she was reading and asked: 'Is the secret session over?'

'Yes.' I moved towards the sofa.

Mimi said: 'Let her sleep awhile, Nick. You're going to stay till after your police friends have gone, aren't you?'

'All right. I want to see Dorothy again.'

'But she's asleep.'

'That's all right. I'll wake her up.'

'But – '

Guild and Andy came in, said their good-nights, Guild looked regretfully at the sleeping Nora, and they left.

Mimi sighed. 'I'm tired of policemen,' she said. 'You remember that story?'

'Yes.'

Gilbert came in. 'Do they really think Chris did it?'

'No,' I said.

'Who do they think?'

'I could've told you yesterday. I can't today.'

'That's ridiculous,' Mimi protested. 'They know very well and you know very well that Clyde did it.' When I said nothing she repeated, more sharply: 'You know very well that Clyde did it.'

'He didn't,' I said.

An expression of triumph brightened Mimi's face. 'You *are* working for him, now aren't you?'

My 'No' bounced off her with no effect whatever.

Gilbert asked, not argumentatively, but as if he wanted to know: 'Why couldn't he?'

'He could've, but he didn't. Would he have written those

letters throwing suspicion on Mimi, the one person who's helping him by hiding the chief evidence against him?'

'But maybe he didn't know that. Maybe he thought the police were simply not telling all they knew. They often do that, don't they? Or maybe he thought he could discredit her, so they wouldn't believe her if – '

'That's it,' Mimi said. 'That's exactly what he did, Nick.'

I said to Gilbert: 'You don't think he killed her.'

'No, I don't think he did, but I'd like to know why you don't think so – you know – your method.'

'And I'd like to know yours.'

His face flushed a little and there was some embarrassment in his smile. 'Oh, but I – it's different.'

'He *knows* who killed her,' Dorothy said from the doorway. She was still dressed. She stared at me fixedly, as if afraid to look at anybody else. Her face was pale and she held her small body stiffly erect.

Nora opened her eyes, pushed herself up on an elbow, and asked: 'What?' sleepily. Nobody answered her.

Mimi said: 'Now, Dorry, don't let's have one of those idiotic dramatic performances.'

Dorothy said: 'You can beat me after they've gone. You will.' She said it without taking her eyes off mine.

Mimi tried to look as if she did not know what her daughter was talking about.

'Who does he know killed her?' I asked.

Gilbert said: 'You're making an ass of yourself, Dorry, you're – '

I interrupted him: 'Let her. Let her say what she's got to say. Who killed her, Dorothy?'

She looked at her brother and lowered her eyes and no longer held herself erect. Looking at the floor, she said indistinctly: 'I don't know. He knows.' She raised her eyes to mine and began to tremble. 'Can't you see I'm afraid?' she cried. 'I'm afraid of them. Take me away and I'll tell you, but I'm afraid of them.'

Mimi laughed at me. 'You asked for it. It serves you right.'

Gilbert was blushing. 'It's so silly,' he mumbled.

I said: 'Sure, I'll take you away, but I'd like to have it out now while we're all together.'

Dorothy shook her head. 'I'm afraid.'

Mimi said: 'I wish you wouldn't baby her so, Nick. It only makes her worse. She – '

I asked Nora: 'What do you say?'

She stood up and stretched without lifting her arms. Her face was pink and lovely as it always is when she has been sleeping. She smiled drowsily at me and said: 'Let's go home. I don't like these people. Come on, get your hat and coat, Dorothy.'

Mimi said to Dorothy: 'Go to bed.'

Dorothy put the tips of the fingers of her left hand to her mouth and whimpered through them: 'Don't let her beat me, Nick.'

I was watching Mimi, whose face wore a placid half-smile, but her nostrils moved with her breathing and I could hear her breathing.

Nora went around to Dorothy. 'Come on, we'll wash your face and – '

Mimi made an animal noise in her throat, muscles thickened on the back of her neck, and she put her weight on the balls of her feet.

Nora stepped between Mimi and Dorothy. I caught Mimi by a shoulder as she started forward, put my other arm round her waist from behind, and lifted her off her feet. She screamed and hit back at me with her fists and her hard sharp high heels made dents in my shins.

Nora pushed Dorothy out of the room and stood in the doorway watching us. Her face was very live. I saw it clearly, sharply: everything else was blurred. When clumsy, ineffectual blows on my back and shoulder brought me around to find Gilbert pommelling me, I could see him but dimly and I hardly felt the contact when I shoved him aside. 'Cut it out. I don't want to hurt you, Gilbert.' I carried Mimi over to the sofa and dumped her on her back on it, sat on her knees, got a wrist in each hand.

Gilbert was at me again. I tried to pop his knee-cap, but kicked him too low, kicked his leg from under him. He went down on the floor in a tangle. I kicked at him again, missed, and said: 'We can fight afterwards. Get some water.'

Mimi's face was becoming purple. Her eyes protruded, glassy, senseless, enormous. Saliva bubbled and hissed between clenched teeth with her breathing, and her red throat – her whole body – was a squirming mass of veins and muscles swollen until it seemed they must burst. Her wrists were hot in my hands and sweat made them hard to hold.

Nora beside me with a glass of water was a welcome sight. 'Chuck it in her face,' I said.

Nora chucked it. Mimi separated her teeth to gasp and she shut her eyes. She moved her head violently from side to side, but there was less violence in the squirming of her body.

'Do it again,' I said.

The second glass of water brought a spluttering protest from Mimi and the fight went out of her body. She lay still limp, panting.

I took my hands away from her wrists and stood up. Gilbert, standing on one foot, was leaning against a table nursing the leg I had kicked. Dorothy, big-eyed and pale, was in the doorway, undecided whether to come in or run off and hide. Nora, beside me, holding the empty glass in her hand, asked: 'Think she's all right?'

'Sure.'

Presently Mimi opened her eyes, tried to blink the water out of them. I put a handkerchief in her hand. She wiped her face, gave a long shivering sigh, and sat up on the sofa. She looked around the room, still blinking a little. When she saw me she smiled feebly. There was guilt in her smile, but nothing you could call remorse. She touched her hair with an unsteady hand and said: 'I've certainly been drowned.'

I said: 'Some day you're going into one of those things and not come out of it.'

She looked past me at her son. 'Gil. What's happened to you?' she asked.

He hastily took his hand off his leg and put his foot down on the floor. 'I – uh – nothing,' he stammered. 'I'm perfectly all right.' He smoothed his hair, straightened his necktie.

She began to laugh. 'Oh, Gil, did you really try to protect me? And from Nick?' Her laughter increased. 'It was awfully sweet of you, but awfully silly. Why, he's a monster, Gil. Nobody could – ' She put my handkerchief over her mouth and rocked back and forth.

I looked sidewise at Nora. Her mouth was set and her eyes were almost black with anger. I touched her arm. 'Let's blow. Give your mother a drink, Gilbert. She'll be all right in a minute or two.'

Dorothy, hat and coat in her hands, tiptoed to the outer door. Nora and I found our hats and coats and followed her out, leaving Mimi laughing into my handkerchief on the sofa.

None of the three of us had much to say in the taxicab that carried us over to the Normandie. Nora was brooding, Dorothy seemed still pretty frightened, and I was tired – it had been a full day.

It was nearly five o'clock when we got home. Asta greeted us boisterously. I lay down on the floor to play with her while Nora went into the pantry to make coffee. Dorothy wanted to tell me something that happened to her when she was a little child.

I said: 'No. You tried that Monday. What is it? A gag? It's late. What was it you were afraid to tell me over there?'

'But you'd understand better if you'd let me – '

'You said *that* Monday. I'm not a psycho-analyst. I don't

know anything about early influences. I don't give a damn about them. And I'm tired – I've been ironing all day.'

She pouted at me. 'You seem to be trying to make it as hard for me as you can.'

'Listen, Dorothy,' I said, 'you either know something you were afraid to say in front of Mimi and Gilbert or you don't. If you do, spit it out. I'll ask you about any of it I find myself not understanding.'

She twisted a fold of her skirt and looked sulkily at it, but when she raised her eyes they became bright and excited. She spoke in a whisper loud enough for anybody in the room to hear: 'Gil's been seeing my father and he saw him today and my father told him who killed Miss Wolf.'

'Who?'

She shook her head. 'He wouldn't tell me. He'd just tell me that.'

'And that's what you were afraid to say in front of Gil and Mimi?'

'Yes. You'd understand that if you'd let me tell you – '

'Something that happened when you were a little child. Well, I won't. Stop it. What else did he tell you?'

'Nothing.'

'Nothing about Nunheim?'

'No, nothing.'

'Where is your father?'

'Gil didn't tell me.'

'When did he meet him?'

'He didn't tell me. Please don't be mad, Nick. I've told you everything he told me.'

'And a fat lot it is,' I growled. 'When'd he tell you this?'

'Tonight. He was telling me when you came in my room, and honest, that's all he told me.'

I said: 'It'd be swell if just once one of you people would make a clear and complete statement about something – it wouldn't matter what.'

Nora came in with the coffee. 'What's worrying you now, son?' she asked.

'Things,' I said, 'riddles, lies, and I'm too old and too tired for them to be any fun. Let's go back to San Francisco.'

'Before New Year's?'

'Tomorrow, today.'

'I'm willing.' She gave me a cup. 'We can fly back, if you want, and be there for New Year's Eve.'

Dorothy said tremulously: 'I didn't lie to you, Nick. I told you everything I – Please, please don't be mad with me. I'm so – ' She stopped talking to sob.

I rubbed Asta's head and groaned.

Nora said: 'We're all worn out and jumpy. Let's send the pup downstairs for the night and turn in and do our talking after we've had some rest. Come on, Dorothy, I'll bring your coffee into the bedroom and give you some night-clothes.'

Dorothy got up, said: 'Good-night,' to me. 'I'm sorry I'm so silly,' and followed Nora out.

When Nora returned she sat down on the floor beside me. 'Our Dorry does her share of weeping and whining,' she said. 'Admitting life's not too pleasant for her just now, still. . . .' She yawned. 'What was her fearsome secret?'

I told her what Dorothy had told me. 'It sounds like a lot of hooey.'

'Why?'

'Why not? Everything else we've got from them has been hooey.'

Nora yawned again. 'That may be good enough for a detective, but it's not convincing enough for me. Listen, why don't we make a list of all the suspects and all the motives and clues, and check them off against – '

'You do it. I'm going to bed. What's a clue, Mamma?'

'It's like when Gilbert tiptoed over to the phone tonight when I was alone in the living-room, and he thought I was asleep, and told the operator not to put through any incoming calls until morning.'

'Well, well.'

'And,' she said, 'it's like Dorothy discovering that she had Aunt Alice's key all the time.'

'Well, well.'

'And it's like Studsy nudging Morelli under the table when he started to tell you about the drunken cousin of – what was it? – Dick O'Brien's that Julia Wolf knew.'

I got up and put our cups on a table. 'I don't see how any detective can hope to get along without being married to you, but, just the same, you're overdoing it. Studsy nudging Morelli is my idea of something to spend a lot of time not worrying about. I'd rather worry about whether they pushed Sparrow around to keep me from being hurt or to keep me from being told something. I'm sleepy.'

XXVI

NORA shook me awake at a quarter past ten. 'The telephone,' she said. 'It's Herbert Macaulay and he says it's important.'

I went into the bedroom – I had slept in the living-room – to the telephone. Dorothy was sleeping soundly. I mumbled: 'Hello,' into the telephone.

Macaulay said: 'It's too early for that lunch, but I've got to see you right away. Can I come up now?'

'Sure. Come up for breakfast.'

'I've had it. Get yours and I'll be up in fifteen minutes.'

'Right.'

Dorothy opened her eyes less than half-way, said: 'It must be late,' sleepily, turned over, and returned to unconsciousness.

I put cold water on my face and hands, brushed my teeth and hair, and went back to the living-room. 'He's coming up,' I told Nora. 'He's had breakfast, but you'd better order some coffee for him. I want chicken livers.'

'Am I invited to your party or do I – '

'Sure. You've never met Macaulay, have you? He's a

pretty good guy. I was attached to his outfit for a few days once, up around Vaux, and we looked each other up after the war. He threw a couple of jobs my way, including the Wynant one. How about a drop of something to cut the phlegm?'

'Why don't you stay sober today?'

'We didn't come to New York to stay sober. Want to see a hockey game tonight?'

'I'd like to.' She poured me a drink and went to order breakfast.

I looked through the morning papers. They had the news of Jorgensen's being picked up by the Boston police and of Nunheim's murder, but further developments of what the tabloids called 'The Hell's Kitchen Gang War', the arrest of 'Prince Mike' Ferguson, and an interview with the 'Jafsie' of the Lindbergh kidnapping negotiations got more space.

Macaulay and the bellboy who brought Asta up arrived together. Asta liked Macaulay because when he patted her he gave her something to set her weight against: she was never very fond of gentleness.

He had lines around his mouth this morning and some of the rosiness was gone from his cheeks. 'Where'd the police get this new line?' he asked. 'Do they think – ' He broke off as Nora came in. She had dressed.

'Nora, this is Herbert Macaulay,' I said. 'My wife.'

They shook hands and Nora said: 'Nick would only let me order some coffee for you. Can I – '

'No thanks, I've just finished breakfast.'

I said: 'Now what's this about the police?'

He hesitated.

'Nora knows practically everything I know,' I assured him, 'so unless it's something you'd rather not – '

'No, no, nothing like that,' he said. 'It's – well – for Mrs Charles's sake. I don't want to cause her anxiety.'

'Then out with it. She only worries about things she doesn't know. What's the new police line?'

143

'Lieutenant Guild came to see me this morning,' he said. 'First he showed me a piece of watch-chain with a knife attached to it and asked me if I'd ever seen them before. I had: they were Wynant's. I told him I thought I had: I thought they looked like Wynant's. Then he asked me if I knew of any way in which they could have come into anybody else's possession and, after some beating about the bush, I discovered that by anybody else he meant you or Mimi. I told him certainly – Wynant could have given them to either of you, you could have stolen them or found them on the street or have been given them by somebody who stole them or found them on the street, or you could have got them from somebody Wynant gave them to. There were other ways, too, for you to have got them, I told him, but he knew I was kidding him, so he wouldn't let me tell him about them.'

There were spots of colour in Nora's cheeks and her eyes were dark. 'The idiot!'

'Now, now,' I said. 'Maybe I should have warned you – he was heading in that direction last night. I think it's likely my old pal Mimi gave him a prod or two. What else did he turn the searchlight on?'

'He wanted to know about – what he asked was: "Do you figure Charles and the Wolf dame was still playing around together? Or was that all washed up?"'

'That's the Mimi touch, all right,' I said. 'What'd you tell him?'

'I told him I didn't know whether you were "still" playing around together because I didn't know that you had ever played around together, and reminded him that you hadn't been living in New York for a long time anyway.'

Nora asked me: 'Did you?'

I said: 'Don't try to make a liar out of Mac. What'd he say to that?'

'Nothing. He asked me if I thought Jorgensen knew about you and Mimi and, when I asked him what about you and Mimi, he accused me of acting the innocent – they were

144

his words – so we didn't get very far. He was interested in the times I had seen you, also, where and when to the exact inch and second.'

'That's nice,' I said. 'I've got lousy alibis.'

A waiter came in with our breakfast. We talked about this and that until he had set the table and gone away.

Then Macaulay said: 'You've nothing to be afraid of. I'm going to turn Wynant over to the police.' His voice was unsteady and a little choked.

'Are you sure he did it?' I asked. 'I'm not.'

He said simply: 'I know.' He cleared his throat. 'Even if there was a chance in a thousand of my being wrong – and there isn't – he's a madman, Charles. He shouldn't be loose.'

'That's probably right enough,' I began, 'and if you know – '

'I know,' he repeated. 'I saw him the afternoon he killed her; it couldn't've been half an hour after he'd killed her, though I didn't know that, didn't even know she'd been killed. I – well – I know it now.'

'You met him in Hermann's office?'

'What?'

'You were supposed to have been in the office of a man named Hermann, on Fifty-seventh Street, from around three o'clock till around four that afternoon. At least, that's what the police told me.'

'That's right,' he said. 'I mean that's the story they got. What really happened: after I failed to find Wynant or any news of him at the Plaza and phoned my office and Julia with no better results, I gave him up and started walking down to Hermann's. He's a mining engineer, a client of mine; I had just finished drawing up some articles of incorporation for him, and there were some minor changes to be made in them. When I got to Fifty-seventh Street I suddenly got a feeling that I was being followed – you know the feeling. I couldn't think of any reason for anybody shadowing me, but still, I'm a lawyer, and there might be.

Anyhow, I wanted to find out, so I turned east on Fifty-seventh and walked over to Madison and still wasn't sure. There was a small sallow man I thought I'd seen around the Plaza, but – The quickest way to find out seemed to be by taking a taxi, so I did that and told the driver to drive east. There was too much traffic there for me to see whether this small man or anybody else took a taxi after me, so I had my driver turn south at Third, east again on Fifty-sixth and south again on Second Avenue, and by that time I was pretty sure a yellow taxi was following me. I couldn't see whether my small man was in it, of course; it wasn't close enough for that. And at the next corner, when a red light stopped us, I saw Wynant. He was in a taxicab going west on Fifty-fifth Street. Naturally, that didn't surprise me very much: we were only two blocks from Julia's and I took it for granted she hadn't wanted me to know he was there when I phoned and that he was now on his way over to meet me at the Plaza. He was never very punctual. So I told my driver to turn west, but at Lexington Avenue – we were half a block behind him – Wynant's taxicab turned south. That wasn't the way to the Plaza and wasn't even the way to my office, so I said to hell with him and turned my attention back to the taxi following me – and it wasn't there any more. I kept a look-out behind all the way over to Hermann's and saw no sign at all of anybody following me.'

'What time was it when you saw Wynant?' I asked.

'It must've been fifteen or twenty minutes past three. It was twenty minutes to four when I got to Hermann's and I imagine that was twenty or twenty-five minutes later. Well, Hermann's secretary – Louise Jacobs, the girl I was with when I saw you last night – told me he had been locked up in a conference all afternoon, but would probably be through in a few minutes, and he was, and I got through with him in ten or fifteen minutes and went back to my office.'

'I take it you weren't close enough to Wynant to see

whether he looked excited, was wearing his watch-chain, smelled of gunpowder – things like that.'

'That's right. All I saw was his profile going past, but don't think I'm not sure it was Wynant.'

'I won't. Go ahead,' I said.

'He didn't phone again. I'd been back about an hour when the police phoned – Julia was dead. Now you must understand that I didn't think Wynant had killed her – not for a minute. You can understand that – you still don't think he did. So when I went over there and the police began to ask me questions about him and I could see they suspected him, I did what ninety-nine out of a hundred lawyers would've done for their clients – I said nothing about having seen him in that neighbourhood at about the time that the murder must have been committed. I told them what I told you – about having the date with him and him not showing up – and let them understand that I had gone over to Hermann's straight from the Plaza.'

'That's understandable enough,' I agreed. 'There was no sense in your saying anything until you had heard his side of the story.'

'Exactly, and, well, the catch is I never heard his side of the story. I'd expected him to show up, phone me, something, but he didn't – until Tuesday, when I got that letter from him from Philadelphia, and there was not a word in it about his failure to meet me Friday, nothing about – but you saw the letter. What'd you think of it?'

'You mean did it sound guilty?'

'Yes.'

'Not particularly,' I said. 'It's about what could be expected from him if he didn't kill her – no great alarm over the police suspecting him except as it might interfere with his work, a desire to have it all cleaned up with no inconvenience to him – not too bright a letter to have come from anybody else, but in line with his particular form of goofiness. I can see him sending it off without the faintest notion that the best thing he could do would be to account for

147

his own actions on the day of the murder. How sure are you he was coming from Julia's when you saw him?'

'I'm sure now. I thought it likely at first. Then I thought he may have been to his shop. It's on First Avenue, just a few blocks from where I saw him, and though it's been closed since he went away, we renewed the lease last month and everything's there waiting for him to come back to it, and he could have been there that afternoon. The police couldn't find anything there to show whether he had or hadn't.'

'I meant to ask you: there was some talk about his having grown whiskers. Was he – '

'No – the same long bony face with the same ragged near-white moustache.'

'Another thing: there was a fellow named Nunheim killed yesterday, a small – '

'I'm coming to that,' he said.

'I was thinking about the little fellow you thought might be shadowing you.'

Macaulay stared at me. 'You mean that might've been Nunheim?'

'I don't know. I was wondering.'

'And I don't know,' he said. 'I never saw Nunheim, far as I – '

'He was a little fellow, not more than five feet three, and would weight maybe a hundred and twenty. I'd say he was thirty-five or -six. Sallow, dark hair and eyes, with the eyes set pretty close together, big mouth, long limp nose, batwing ears – shifty looking.'

'That could easily be him,' he said, 'though I didn't get too close a view of my man. I suppose the police would let me see him' – he shrugged – 'not that it matters now. Where was I? Oh, yes, about not being able to get in touch with Wynant. That put me in an uncomfortable position, since the police clearly thought I was in touch with him and lying about it. So did you, didn't you?'

'Yes,' I admitted.

'And you *also*, like the police, probably suspected that I *had* met him, either at the Plaza or later, on the day of the murder.'

'It seemed possible.'

'Yes. And of course you were partly right. I had at least seen him, and seen him at a place and time that would've spelled Guilty with a capital G to the police, so, having lied instinctively and by inference, I now lied directly and deliberately. Hermann had been tied up in a conference all that afternoon and didn't know how long I had been waiting to see him. Louise Jacobs is a good friend of mine. Without going into details, I told her she could help me help a client by saying I had arrived there at a minute or two after three o'clock and she agreed readily enough. To protect her in case of trouble, I told her that if anything went wrong she could always say that she hadn't remembered what time I arrived, but that I, the next day, had casually mentioned my arrival at that time and she had no reason for doubting me – throwing the whole thing on me.' Macaulay took a deep breath. 'None of that's important now. What's important is that I heard from Wynant this morning.'

'Another one of those screwy letters?' I asked.

'No, he phoned. I made a date with him for tonight – for you and me. I told him you wouldn't do anything for him unless you could see him, so he promised to meet us tonight. I'm going to take the police, of course; I can't go on justifying my shielding him like this. I can get him an acquittal on grounds of insanity and have him put away. That's all I can do, all I want to do.'

'Have you told the police yet?'

'No. He didn't phone till just after they'd left. Anyway, I wanted to see you first. I wanted to tell you I hadn't forgotten what I owed you and – '

'Nonsense,' I said.

'It's not.' He turned to Nora. 'I don't suppose he ever told you he saved my life once in a shell-hole in – '

'He's nuts,' I told her. 'He fired at a fellow and missed and I fired at him and didn't and that's all there was to it.' I addressed him again: 'Why don't you let the police wait awhile? Suppose you and I keep this date tonight and hear what he's got to say. We can sit on him and blow whistles when the meeting's about to break up if we're convinced he's the murderer.'

Macaulay smiled wearily. 'You're still doubtful, aren't you? Well, I'm willing to do it that way if you want, though it seems like a – But perhaps you'll change your mind when I tell you about our telephone conversation.

Dorothy, wearing a nightgown and a robe of Nora's, both much too long for her, came in yawning. 'Oh!' she exclaimed when she saw Macaulay, and then, when she had recognized him: 'Oh, hello, Mr Macaulay. I didn't know you were here. Is there any news of my father?'

He looked at me. I shook my head. He told her: 'Not yet, but perhaps we'll have some today.'

I said: 'Dorothy's had some, indirectly. Tell Macaulay about Gilbert.'

'You mean about – about my father?' she asked hesitantly, staring at the floor.

'Oh, dear me, no,' I said.

Her face flushed and she glanced reproachfully at me; then, hastily, she told Macaulay: 'Gil saw my father yesterday and he told Gil who killed Miss Wolf.'

'What?'

She nodded four or five times, earnestly.

Macaulay looked at me with puzzled eyes.

'This doesn't have to've happened,' I reminded him. 'It's what Gil says happened.'

'I see. Then you think he might be – ?'

'You haven't done much talking to that family since hell broke loose, have you?' I asked.

'No.'

'It's an experience. They're all sex-crazy, I think, and it backs up into their heads. They start off – '

150

Dorothy said angrily: 'I think you're horrid. I've done my best to – '

'What are you kicking about?' I demanded. 'I'm giving you the break this time: I'm willing to believe Gil did tell you that. Don't expect too much of me.'

Macaulay asked: 'And who killed her?'

'I don't know. Gil wouldn't tell me.'

'Had your brother seen him often?'

'I don't know how often. He said he had been seeing him.'

'And was anything said – well – about the man Nunheim?'

'No. Nick asked me that. He didn't tell me anything else at all.'

I caught Nora's eye and made signals. She stood up saying: 'Let's go in the other room, Dorothy, and give these lads a chance to do whatever it is they think they're doing.'

Dorothy went reluctantly, but she went out with Nora.

Macaulay said: 'She's grown up to be something to look at.' He cleared his throat. 'I hope your wife won't – '

'Forget it. Nora's all right. You started to tell me about your conversation with Wynant.'

'He phoned right after the police left and said he'd seen the ad. in the *Times* and wanted to know what I wanted. I told him you weren't anxious to get yourself mixed up in his troubles and had said you wouldn't touch it at all without talking it over with him first, and we made the date for tonight. Then he asked if I'd seen Mimi and I told him I'd seen her once or twice since her return from Europe and had also seen his daughter. And then he said this: "If my wife should ask for money, give her any sum in reason".'

'I'll be damned,' I said.

Macaulay nodded. 'That's the way I felt about it. I asked him why and he said what he'd read in the morning papers had convinced him that she was Rosewater's dupe, not his confederate, and he had reason to believe she was "kindly disposed" towards him, Wynant. I began to see what he was up to, then, and I told him she had already turned the knife and chain over to the police. And try to guess what he said to that.'

'I give up.'

'He hemmed and hawed a bit – not much, mind you – and then as smooth as you like asked: "You mean the chain and knife on the watch I left with Julia to be repaired?"'

I laughed. 'What'd you say?'

'That stumped me. Before I could think up an answer he was saying: "However, we can discuss that more fully when we meet tonight." I asked him where and when we'd meet him and he said he'd have to phone me, he didn't know where he'd be. He's to phone me at my house at ten o'clock. He was in a hurry now, though he had seemed leisurely enough before, and hadn't time to answer any of the things I wanted to ask, so he hung up and I phoned you. What do you think of his innocence now?'

'Not so much as I did,' I replied slowly. 'How sure are you of hearing from him at ten tonight?'

Macaulay shrugged. 'You know as much about that as I do.'

'Then if I were you I wouldn't bother the police till we've grabbed our wild man and can turn him over to them. This story of yours isn't going to make them exactly love you and, even if they don't throw you in the can right away, they'll make things pretty disagreeable for you if Wynant gives us a run-around tonight.'

'I know, but I'd like to get the load off my shoulders.'

'A few hours more oughtn't to matter much,' I said. 'Did either of you say anything about his not keeping the date at the Plaza?'

'No. I didn't get a chance to ask him. Well, if you say wait, I'll wait, but – '

'Let's wait till tonight, anyhow, till he phones you – if

he does – and then we can make up our minds whether to take the police along.'

'You don't think he'll phone?'

'I'm not too sure,' I said. 'He didn't keep his last date with you, and he seems to have gone pretty vague on you as soon as he learned that Mimi had turned in the watch-chain and knife. I wouldn't be too optimistic about it. We'll see, though. I'd better get out to your house at about nine o'clock, hadn't I?'

'Come for dinner.'

'I can't, but I'll make it as early as I can, in case he's ahead of time. We'll want to move fast. Where do you live?'

Macaulay gave me his address, in Scarsdale, and stood up. 'Will you say good-bye to Mrs Charles for me and thank – Oh, by the way, I hope you didn't misunderstand me about Harrison Quinn last night. I meant only just what I said, that I'd had bad luck taking his advice on the market. I didn't mean to insinuate that there was anything – you know – or that he might not've made money for his other customers.'

'I understand,' I said, and called Nora.

She and Macaulay shook hands and made polite speeches to each other and he pushed Asta around a little and said: 'Make it as early as you can,' to me and went away.

'There goes the hockey game,' I said, 'unless you find somebody else to go with.'

'Did I miss anything?' Nora asked.

'Not much.' I told her what Macaulay had told me. 'And don't ask me what I think of it. I don't know. I know Wynant's crazy, but he's not acting like a crazy man and he's not acting like a murderer. He's acting like a man playing some kind of game. God only knows what the game is.'

'I think,' she said, 'that he's shielding somebody else.'

'Why don't you think he did it?'

She looked surprised. 'Because you don't.'

153

I said that was a swell reason. 'Who is the somebody else?'

'I don't know yet. Now don't make fun of me: I've thought about it a lot. It wouldn't be Macaulay, because he's using him to help shield whoever it is and – '

'And it wouldn't be me,' I suggested, 'because he wants to use me.'

'That's right,' she said, 'and you're going to feel very silly if you make fun of me and then I guess who it is before you do. And it wouldn't be either Mimi or Jorgensen, because he tried to throw suspicion on them. And it wouldn't be Nunheim, because he was most likely killed by the same person and, furthermore, wouldn't have to be shielded now. And it wouldn't be Morelli, because Wynant was jealous of him and they'd had a row.' She frowned at me. 'I wish you'd found out more about that big fat man they called Sparrow and that big red-haired woman.'

'But how about Dorothy and Gilbert?'

'I wanted to ask you about them. Do you think he's got any very strong paternal feeling for them?'

'No.'

'You're probably just trying to discourage me,' she said. 'Well, knowing them, it's hard to think either of them might've been guilty, but I tried to throw out my personal feelings and stick to logic. Before I went to sleep last night I made a list of all the – '

'There's nothing like a little logic-sticking to ward off insomnia. It's like – '

'Don't be so damned patronizing. Your performance so far has been a little less than dazzling.'

'I didn't mean no harm,' I said and kissed her. 'That a new dress?'

'Ah! Changing the subject, you coward.'

XXVII

I WENT to see Guild early in the afternoon and went to
work on him as soon as we had shaken hands. 'I didn't
bring my lawyer along. I thought it looked better if I came
by myself.'

He wrinkled his forehead and shook his head as if I had
hurt him. 'Now it was nothing like that,' he said patiently.

'It was too much like that.'

He sighed. 'I wouldn't've thought you'd make the mistake
that a lot of people make thinking just because we – You
know we got to look at every angle, Mr Charles.'

'That sounds familiar. Well, what do you want to know?'

'All I want to know is who killed her – and him.'

'Try asking Gilbert,' I suggested.

Guild pursed his lips. 'Why him exactly?'

'He told his sister he knew who did it, told her he got
it from Wynant.'

'You mean he's been seeing the old man?'

'So she says he said. I haven't had a chance to ask him
about it.'

He squinted his watery eyes at me. 'Just what is that lay-
out over there, Mr Charles?'

'The Jorgensen family? You probably know as much
about it as I do.'

'I don't,' he said, 'and that's a fact. I just can't size them
up at all. This Mrs Jorgensen, now, what is she?'

'A blonde.'

He nodded gloomily. 'Uh-huh, and that's all I know. But
look, you've known them a long time and from what she
says you and her – '

'And me and her daughter,' I said, 'and me and
Julia Wolf and me and Mrs Astor. I'm hell with the
women.'

He held up a hand. 'I'm not saying I believe everything
she says, and there's nothing to get sore about. You're

taking the wrong attitude, if you don't mind me saying it. You're acting like you thought we were out to get you, and that's all wrong, absolutely all wrong.'

'Maybe, but you've been talking double to me ever since last – '

He looked at me with steady pale eyes and said calmly: 'I'm a copper and I got my work to do.'

'That's reasonable enough. You told me to come in today. What do you want?'

'I didn't tell you to come in, I asked you.'

'All right. What do you want?'

'I don't want this,' he said. 'I don't want anything like this. We've been talking man to man up to this time and I'd kind of like to go on that way.'

'You made the change.'

'I don't think that's a fact. Look here, Mr Charles, would you take your oath, or even just tell me straight out, that you've been emptying your pockets to me right along?'

There was no use saying yes – he would not have believed me. I said: 'Practically.'

'Practically, yes,' he grumbled. 'Everybody's been telling me practically the whole truth. What I want's some impractical son of a gun that'll shoot the works.'

I could sympathize with him: I knew how he felt. I said: 'Maybe nobody you've found knows the whole truth.'

He made an unpleasant face. 'That's very likely, ain't it? Listen, Mr Charles. I've talked to everybody I could find. If you can find any more for me, I'll talk to them too. You mean Wynant? Don't you suppose we got every facility the department's got working night and day trying to turn him up?'

'There's his son,' I suggested.

'There's his son,' he agreed. He called in Andy and a swarthy bow-legged man named Kline. 'Get me that Wynant kid – the punk – I want to talk to him.' They went out. He said: 'See, I want people to talk to.'

I said: 'Your nerves are in pretty bad shape this after-

156

noon, aren't they? Are you bringing Jorgensen down from Boston?'

He shrugged his big shoulders. 'His story listens all right to me. I don't know. Want to tell me what you think of it?'

'Sure.'

'I'm kind of jumpy this afternoon, for a fact,' he said. 'I didn't get a single solitary wink of sleep last night. It's a hell of a life. I don't know why I stick at it. A fellow can get a piece of land and some wire fencing and a few head of silver fox and – Well, anyways, when you people scared Jorgensen off back in '25, he says he lit out for Germany, leaving his wife in the lurch – though he don't say much about that – and changing his name to give you more trouble finding him, and on the same account he's afraid to work at his regular job – he calls himself some kind of a technician or something – so pickings are kind of slim. He says he worked at one thing and another, whatever he could get, but near as I can figure out he was mostly gigoloing, if you know what I mean, and not finding too many heavy money dames. Well, along about '27 or '28 he's in Milan – that's a city in Italy – and he sees in the Paris *Herald* where this Mimi, recently divorced wife of Clyde Miller Wynant, has arrived in Paris. He don't know her personally and she don't know him, but he knows she's a dizzy blonde that likes men and fun and hasn't got much sense. He figures a bunch of Wynant's dough must've come to her with the divorce and, the way he looks at it, any of it he could take away from her wouldn't be any more than what Wynant had gypped him out of – he'd only be getting some of what belonged to him. So he scrapes up the fare to Paris and goes up there. All right so far?'

'Sounds all right.'

'That's what I thought. Well, he don't have any trouble getting to know her in Paris – either picking her up or getting somebody to introduce him or whatever happened – and the rest of it's just as easy. She goes for him in a big way – bing, according to him – right off the bat, and the first thing you know she's one jump ahead of him, she's thinking about marrying him. Naturally he don't try to talk her out of that. She'd gotten a lump sum – two hundred thousand berries, by God! – out of Wynant instead of alimony, so her marrying again wasn't stopping any payments, and it'll put him right in the middle of the cash-drawer. So they do it. According to him, it was a trick marriage up in some mountains he says are between Spain and France and was done by a Spanish priest on what was really French soil, which don't make it legal, but I figure he's just trying to discourage a bigamy rap. Personally, I don't care one way or the other. The point is he got his hands on the dough and kept them on it till there wasn't any more dough. And all this time, understand, he says she didn't know he was anybody but Christian Jorgensen, a fellow she met in Paris, and still didn't know it up to the time we grabbed him in Boston. Still sound all right?'

'Still sounds all right,' I said, 'except, as you say, about the marriage, and even that could be all right.'

'Uh-huh, and what difference does it make anyways? So comes the winter and the bank-roll's getting skinny and he's getting ready to take a run-out on her with the last of it, and then she says maybe they could come back to America and tap Wynant for some more. He thinks that's fair enough if it can be done, and she thinks it can be done, so they get on a boat and – '

'The story cracks a little there,' I said.

'What makes you think so? He's not figuring on going to Boston, where he knows his first wife is, and he's figuring on keeping out of the way of the few people that know him, including especially Wynant, and somebody's told him there's a statute of limitation making everything just lovely after seven years. He don't figure he's running much risk. They ain't going to stay here long.'

'I still don't like that part of his story,' I insisted, 'but go ahead.'

'Well, the second day he's here – while they're still trying to find Wynant – he gets a bad break. He runs into a friend of his first wife's – this Olga Fenton – on the street and she recognizes him. He tries to talk her out of tipping off the first wife and does manage to stall her along a couple days with a moving-picture story he makes up – what an imagination that guy's got! – but he don't fool her long, and she goes to her parson and tells him about it and asks him what she ought to do and he says she ought to tell the first wife, and so she does, and the next time she sees Jorgensen she tells him what she's done, and he lights out for Boston to try to keep his wife from kicking up trouble and we pick him up there.'

'How about his visit to the hock-shop?' I asked.

'That was part of it. He says there was a train for Boston leaving in a few minutes and he didn't have any dough with him and didn't have time to go home for some – besides not being anxious to face the second wife till he had the first one quieted down – and the banks were closed, so he soaked his watch. It checks up.'

'Did you see the watch?'

'I can. Why?'

'I was wondering. You don't think it was once on the other end of that piece of chain Mimi turned over to you?'

He sat up straight. 'By God!' Then he squinted at me suspiciously and asked: 'Do you know anything about it or are you – '

'No. I was just wondering. What does he say about the murders now? Who does he think did them?'

'Wynant. He admits for a while he thought Mimi might've, but he says she convinced him different. He claims she wouldn't tell him what she had on Wynant. He might be just trying to cover himself up on that. I don't guess there's any doubt about them meaning to use it to shake him down for that money they wanted.'

'Then you don't think she planted the knife and chain?'

Guild pulled down the ends of his mouth. 'She could've

planted them to shake him down with. What's wrong with that?'

'It's a little complicated for a fellow like me,' I said. 'Find out if Face Peppler's still in the Ohio pen?'

'Uh-huh. He gets out next week. That accounts for the diamond ring. He had a pal of his on the outside send it to her for him. Seems they were planning to get married and go straight together after he got out, or some such. Anyways, the warden says he saw letters passing between them reading like that. This Peppler won't tell the warden that he knows anything that'll help us, and the warden don't call to mind anything that was in their letters that's any good to us. Of course, even this much helps some, with the motive. Say Wynant's jealous and she's wearing this other guy's ring and getting ready to go away with him. That'll – ' He broke off to answer his telephone. 'Yes,' he said into it. 'Yes . . . what? . . . Sure . . . Sure, but leave somebody there . . . That's right.' He pushed the telephone aside. 'Another bum steer on that west Twenty-ninth Street killing yesterday.'

'Oh,' I said. 'I thought I heard Wynant's name. You know how some telephone voices carry.'

He blushed, cleared his throat. 'Maybe something sounded like it – why not, I guess. Uh-huh, that could sound like it – *why not*. I almost forgot: we looked up that fellow Sparrow for you.'

'What'd you find out?'

'It looks like there's nothing there for us. His name's Jim Brophy. It figures out that he was making a play for that girl at Nunheim's and she was sore at you and he was just drunk enough to think he could put himself in solid with her by taking a poke at you.'

'A nice idea,' I said. 'I hope you didn't make any trouble for Studsy.'

'A friend of yours? He's an ex-con, you know, with a record as long as your arm.'

'Sure. I sent him over once.' I started to gather up my hat and overcoat. 'You're busy. I'll run along and – '

'No, no,' he said. 'Stick around if you got the time. I got a couple of things coming in that'll maybe interest you, and you can give me a hand with that Wynant kid, too, maybe.' I sat down again.

'Maybe you'd like a drink,' he suggested, opening a drawer of his desk, but I had never had much luck with policemen's liquor, so I said: 'No thanks.'

His telephone rang again and he said into it: 'Yes ... Yes ... That's all right. Come on in.' This time no words leaked out to me.

He rocked back in his chair and put his feet on his desk, 'Listen, I'm on the level about that silver fox farming and I want to ask you what you think of California for a place.'

I was trying to decide whether to tell him about the lion and ostrich farms in the lower part of the state when the door opened and a fat, red-haired man brought Gilbert Wynant in. One of Gilbert's eyes was completely shut by swollen flesh around it and his left knee showed through a tear in his pants-leg.

XXVIII

I SAID to Guild: 'When you say bring 'em in, they bring 'em in, don't they?'

'Wait,' he told me. 'This is more'n you think.' He addressed the fat, red-haired man: 'Go ahead, Flint, let's have it.'

Flint wiped his mouth with the back of a hand. 'He's a wildcat for fair, the young fellow. He don't look tough, but, man, he didn't want to come along, I can tell you that. And can he run!'

Guild growled: 'You're a hero and I'll see the Commissioner about your medal right away, but never mind that now. Talk turkey.'

'I wasn't saying I did anything great,' Flint protested. 'I was just – '

161

'I don't give a damn what you did,' Guild said. 'I want to know what he did.'

'Yes, sir, I was getting to that. I relieved Morgan at eight o'clock this morning and everything went along smooth and quiet as per usual, with not a creature was stirring, as the fellow says, till along about ten minutes after two, and then what do I hear but a key in the lock.' He sucked in his lips and gave us a chance to express our amazement.

'The Wolf dame's apartment,' Guild explained to me. 'I had a hunch.'

'And what a hunch!' Flint exclaimed, practically top-heavy with admiration. 'Man, what a hunch!' Guild glared at him and he went on hastily: 'Yes, sir, a key, and then the door opens and this young fellow comes in.' He grinned proudly, affectionately, at Gilbert. 'Scared stiff, he looked, and when I went for him he was out and away like a streak and it wasn't till the first floor that I caught him, and then, by golly, he put up a tussle and I had to bat him in the eye to tone him down. He don't look tough, but – '

'What'd he do in the apartment?' Guild asked.

'He didn't have a chance to do nothing. I – '

'You mean you jumped him without waiting to see what he was up to?' Guild's neck bulged over the edge of his collar, and his face was as red as Flint's hair.

'I thought it was best not to take no chances.'

Guild stared at me with angry incredulous eyes. I did my best to keep my face blank. He said in a choking voice: 'That'll do, Flint. Wait outside.'

The red-haired man seemed puzzled. He said: 'Yes, sir,' slowly. 'Here's his key.' He put the key on Guild's desk and went to the door. There he twisted his head over a shoulder to say: 'He claims he's Clyde Wynant's son.' He laughed merrily.

Guild, still having trouble with his voice, said: 'Oh, he does, does he?'

'Yeah. I seen him somewhere before. I got an idea he

used to belong to Big Shorty Dolan's mob. Seems to me I used to see him around – '

'Get out!' Guild snarled, and Flint got out. Guild groaned from deep down in his big body. 'That mug gets me. Big Shorty Dolan's mob!' He shook his head hopelessly and addressed Gilbert: 'Well, son?'

Gilbert said: 'I know I shouldn't've done it.'

'That's a fair start,' Guild said genially. His face was becoming normal again. 'We all make mistakes. Pull yourself up a chair and let's see what we can do about getting you out of the soup. Want anything for that eye?'

'No, thank you, it's quite all right.' Gilbert moved a chair two or three inches towards Guild and sat down.

'Did that bum smack you just to be doing something?'

'No, no, it was my fault. I – I did resist.'

'Oh, well,' Guild said, 'nobody likes to be arrested, I guess. Now what's the trouble?'

Gilbert looked at me with his one good eye.

'You're in as bad a hole as Lieutenant Guild wants to put you,' I told him. 'You'll make it easy for yourself by making it easy for him.'

Guild nodded earnestly. 'And that's a fact.' He settled himself comfortably in his chair and asked, in a friendly tone: 'Where'd you get the key?'

'My father sent it to me in his letter.' He took a white envelope from his pocket and gave it to Guild.

I went around behind Guild and looked at the envelope over his shoulder. The address was typewritten, *Mr Gilbert Wynant, The Courtla..d*, and there was no postage stamp stuck on it.

'When'd you get it?' I asked.

'It was at the desk when I got in last night, around ten o'clock. I didn't ask the clerk how long it had been there, but I don't suppose it was there when I went out with you, or they'd have given it to me.'

Inside the envelope were two sheets of paper covered with the familiar unskilful typewriting. Guild and I read together:

DEAR GILBERT:

If all these years have gone by without my having communicated with you, it is only because your mother wished it so and if now I break this silence with a request for your assistance it is because only great need could make me go against your mother's wishes. Also you are a man now and I feel that you yourself are the one to decide whether or not we should go on being strangers or whether we should act in accordance with our ties of blood. That I am in an embarrassing situation now in connexion with Julia Wolf's so-called murder I think you know and I trust that you still have remaining enough affection for me to at least hope that I am in all ways guiltless of any complicity therein, which is indeed the case. I turn to you now for help in demonstrating my innocence once and for all to the police and to the world with every confidence that even could I not count on your affection for me I nevertheless could count on your natural desire to do anything within your power to keep unblemished the name that is yours and your sister's as well as your Father's. I turn to you also because while I have a lawyer who is able and who believes in my innocence and who is leaving no stone unturned to prove it and have hopes of engaging Mr Nick Charles to assist him I cannot ask either of them to undertake what is after all a patently illegal act nor do I know anybody else except you that I dare confide in. What I wish you to do is this, tomorrow go to Julia Wolf's apartment at 411 East 54th St to which the enclosed key will admit you and between the pages of a book called *The Grand Manner* you will find a certain paper or statement which you are to read and destroy immediately. You are to be sure you destroy it completely leaving not so much as an ash and when you have read it you will know why this must be done and will understand why I have entrusted this task to you. In the event that something should develop to make a change in our plans advisable I will call you on the telephone late tonight. If you do not hear from me I will telephone you tomorrow evening to learn if you have carried out my instructions and to make arrangements for a meeting. I have every confidence that you will realize the tremendous responsibility I am placing on your shoulders and that my confidence is not misplaced.

Affectionately,

YOUR FATHER

164

Wynant's sprawling signature was written in ink beneath 'Your Father'.

Guild waited for me to say something. I waited for him. After a little of that he asked Gilbert: 'And did he phone?'

'No, sir.'

'How do you know?' I asked. 'Didn't you tell the operator not to put any calls through?'

'I – yes, I did. I was afraid you'd find out who it was if he called up while you were there, but he'd've left some kind of message with the operator, I think, and he didn't.'

'Then you haven't been seeing him?'

'No.'

'And he didn't tell you who killed Julia Wolf?'

'No.'

'You were lying to Dorothy?'

He lowered his head and nodded at the floor. 'I was – it was – I suppose it was jealousy really.' He looked up at me now and his face was pink. 'You see, Dorry used to look up to me and think I knew more than anybody else about almost everything and – you know – she'd come to me if there was anything she wanted to know and she always did what I told her, and then, when she got seeing you, it was different. She looked up to you and respected you more – she naturally would, I mean, she'd've been silly if she hadn't, because there's no comparison, of course, but I – I suppose I was jealous and resented – well, not exactly resented it, because I looked up to you too – but I wanted to do something to impress her again – show off, I guess you'd call it – and when I got that letter I pretended I'd been seeing my father and he'd told me who committed those murders, so she'd think I knew things even you didn't.' He stopped, out of breath, and wiped his face with a handkerchief.

I outwaited Guild again until presently he said: 'Well, I guess there ain't been a great deal of harm done, sonny, if you're sure you ain't doing harm by holding back some other things we ought to know.'

The boy shook his head. 'No, sir, I'm not holding back anything.'

'You don't know anything about that knife and chain your mother give us?'

'No, sir, and I didn't know a thing about it till after she had given it to you.'

'How is she?' I asked.

'Oh, she's all right, I think, though she said she was going to stay in bed today.'

Guild narrowed his eyes. 'What's the matter with her?'

'Hysteria,' I told him. 'She and the daughter had a row last night and she blew up.'

'A row about what?'

'God knows – one of those feminine brain-storms.'

Guild said: 'Hm-m-m,' and scratched his chin.

'Was Flint right in saying you didn't get a chance to hunt for your paper?' I asked the boy.

'Yes. I hadn't even had time to shut the door when he ran at me.'

'They're grand detectives I got working for me,' Guild growled. 'Didn't he yell, "Boo!" when he jumped out at you? Never mind. Well, son, I can do one of two things, and the which depends on you. I can hold you for a while or I can let you go in exchange for a promise that you'll let me know as soon as your father gets in touch with you and let me know what he tells you and where he wants you to meet him, if any.'

I spoke before Gilbert could speak: 'You can't ask that of him, Guild. It's his own father.'

'I can't, huh?' He scowled at me. 'Ain't it for his father's good if he's innocent?'

I said nothing.

Guild's face cleared slowly. 'All right, then, son, suppose I put you on a kind of parole. If your father or anybody else asks you to do anything, will you promise to tell them you can't because you give me your word of honour you wouldn't?'

I said: 'That sounds reasonable.'

Gilbert said: 'Yes, sir, I'll give you my word.'

Guild made a large gesture with one hand. 'Oke. Run along.'

The boy stood up saying: 'Thank you very much, sir.' He turned to me. 'Are you going to be – '

'Wait for me outside,' I told him, 'if you're not in a hurry.'

'I will. Good-bye, Lieutenant Guild, and thank you.' He went out.

Guild grabbed his telephone and ordered *The Grand Manner* and its contents found and brought to him. That done, he clasped his hands behind his head and rocked back in his chair. 'So what?'

'It's anybody's guess,' I said.

'Look here, you don't still think Wynant didn't do it?'

'What difference does it make what I think? You've got plenty on him now with what Mimi gave you.'

'It makes a lot of difference,' he assured me. 'I'd like a lot to know what you think and why.'

'My wife thinks he's trying to cover up somebody else.'

'Is that so? Hm-m-m. I was never one to belittle women's intuition and, if you don't mind me saying so, Mrs Charles is a mighty smart woman. Who does she think it is?'

'She hadn't decided, the last I heard.'

He sighed. 'Well, maybe that paper he sent the kid for will tell us something.'

But the paper told us nothing that afternoon: Guild's men ould not find it, could not find a copy of *The Grand Mann* n the dead woman's room.

XXIX

GUILD had red-haired Flint in again and put the thumb-screws on him. The red-haired man sweated away ten pounds, but he stuck to it that Gilbert had had no opportunity to disturb anything in the apartment and throughout Flint's guardianship nobody hadn't touched nothing. He did not remember having seen a book called *The Grand Manner*, but he was not a man you would expect to memorize book titles. He tried to be helpful and made idiotic suggestions until Guild chased him out.

'The kid's probably waiting for me outside,' I said, 'if you think talking to him again will do any good.'

'Do you?'

'No.'

'Well, then. But, by God, somebody took that book and I'm going to – '

'Why?' I asked.

'Why what?'

'Why'd it have to be there for somebody to take?'

Guild scratched his chin. 'Just what do you mean by that?'

'He didn't meet Macaulay at the Plaza the day of the murder, he didn't commit suicide in Allentown, he says he only got a thousand from Julia Wolf when we thought he was getting five thousand, he says they were just friends when we think they were lovers, he disappoints us too much for me to have much confidence in what he says.'

'It's a fact,' Guild said, 'that I'd understand it better if he'd either come in or run away. Him hanging around like this, just messing things up, don't fit in anywheres that I can see.'

'Are you watching his shop?'

'We're kind of keeping an eye on it. Why?'

'I don't know,' I said truthfully, 'except that he's pointed his finger at a lot of things that got us nowhere. Maybe we ought to pay some attention to the things he hasn't pointed at, and the shop's one of them.'

Guild said: 'Hm-m-m.'

I said: 'I'll leave you with that bright thought,' and put on my hat and coat. 'Suppose I wanted to get hold of you late at night, how would I reach you?'

He gave me his telephone number, we shook hands, and I left.

Gilbert Wynant was waiting for me in the corridor. Neither of us said anything until we were in a taxicab. Then he asked: 'He thinks I was telling the truth, doesn't he?'

'Sure. Weren't you?'

'Oh, yes, but people don't always believe you. You won't say anything to Mamma about this, will you?'

'Not if you don't want me to.'

'Thank you,' he said. 'In your opinion, is there more opportunity for a young man out West than here in the East?'

I thought of him working on Guild's fox farm while I replied: 'Not now. Thinking of going west?'

'I don't know. I want to do something.' He fidgeted with his necktie.

We had a couple of blocks of silence after that. Then he said: 'There's another funny question I'd like to ask you: what do you think of me?' He was more self-conscious about it than Alice Quinn had been.

'You're all right,' I told him, 'and you're all wrong.'

He looked away, out the window. 'I'm so awfully young.'

We had some more silence. Then he coughed and a little blood trickled from one corner of his mouth.

'That guy did hurt you,' I said.

He nodded shamefacedly and put his handkerchief to his mouth. 'I'm not very strong.'

At the Courtland he would not let me help him out of the taxicab and he insisted he could manage alone, but I went upstairs with him, suspecting that otherwise he would say nothing to anybody about his condition.

I rang the apartment bell before he could get his key out, and Mimi opened the door. She goggled at his black eye.

I said: 'He's hurt. Get him to bed and get him a doctor.'

'What happened?'

'Wynant sent him into something.'

'Into what?'

'Never mind that until we get him fixed up.'

'But Clyde was here,' she said. 'That's why I phoned you.'

'What?'

'He was.' She nodded vigorously. 'And he asked where Gil was. He was here for an hour or more. He hasn't been gone ten minutes.'

'All right, let's get him to bed.'

Gilbert stubbornly insisted that he needed no help, so I left him in the bedroom with his mother and went out to the telephone.

'Any calls?' I asked Nora when I had her on the line.

'Yes, sir. Messrs Macaulay and Guild want you to phone them, and Mesdames Jorgensen and Quinn want you to phone them. No children so far.'

'When did Guild call?'

'About five minutes ago. Mind eating alone? Larry asked me to go to see the new Osgood Perkins show with him.'

'Go ahead. See you later.'

I called up Herbert Macaulay.

'The date's off,' he told me. 'I heard from our friend and he's up to God knows what. Listen, Charles, I'm going to the police. I've had enough of it.'

'I guess there's nothing else to do now,' I said. 'I was thinking about telephoning some policemen myself. I'm at Mimi's. He was here a few minutes ago. I just missed him.'

'What was he doing there?'

'I'm going to try and find out now.'

'Were you serious about phoning the police?'

'Sure.'

'Then suppose you do that and I'll come on over.'

'Right. Be seeing you.'

I called up Guild.

'A little news came in right after you left,' he said. 'Are you where I can give it to you?'

'I'm at Mrs Jorgensen's. I had to bring the kid home. That red-head lad of yours has got him bleeding somewhere inside.'

'I'll kill that mug,' he snarled. 'Then I better not talk.'

'I've got some news, too. Wynant was here for about an hour this afternoon, according to Mrs Jorgensen, and left only a few minutes before I got here.'

There was a moment of silence, then he said: 'Hold everything. I'll be right up.'

Mimi came into the living-room while I was looking up the Quinns' telephone number. 'Do you think he's seriously hurt?' she asked.

'I don't know, but you ought to get your doctor right away.' I pushed the telephone towards her. When she was through with it, I said: 'I told the police Wynant had been here.'

She nodded. 'That's what I telephoned you for, to ask if I ought to tell them.'

'I phoned Macaulay, too. He's coming over.'

'He can't do anything,' she said indignantly. 'Clyde gave them to me of his own free will – they're mine.'

'What's yours?'

'Those bonds; the money.'

'What bonds? What money?'

She went to the table and pulled the drawer out. 'See?'

Inside were three packages of bonds held together by thick rubber bands. Across the top of them lay a pink cheque on the Park Avenue Trust Company to the order of Mimi Jorgensen for ten thousand dollars, signed Clyde Miller Wynant, and dated January 3, 1933.

'Dated five days ahead,' I said. 'What kind of nonsense is that?'

'He said he hadn't that much in his account and might not be able to make a deposit for a couple of days.'

'There's going to be hell about this,' I warned her. 'I hope you're ready for it.'

'I don't see why,' she protested. 'I don't see why my

171

husband – my former husband – can't provide for me and his children if he wants to.'

'Cut it out. What'd you sell him?'

'Sell him?'

'Uh-huh. What'd you promise to do in the next few days or he fixes it so the cheque's no good?'

She made an impatient face. 'Really, Nick, I think you're a half-wit sometimes with your silly suspicions.'

'I'm studying to be one. Three more lessons and I get my diploma. But remember I warned you yesterday that you'll probably wind up in – '

'Stop it,' she cried. She put a hand over my mouth. 'Do you have to keep saying that? You know it terrifies me and – ' Her voice became soft and wheedling. 'You must know what I'm going through these days, Nick. Can't you be a little kinder?'

'Don't worry about me,' I said. 'Worry about the police.' I went back to the telephone and called up Alice Quinn. 'This is Nick. Nora said you – '

'Yes. Have you seen Harrison?'

'Not since I left him with you.'

'Well, if you do, you won't say anything about what I said last night, will you? I didn't mean it, really I didn't mean a word of it.'

'I didn't think you did,' I assured her, 'and I wouldn't say anything about it anyway. How's he feeling today?'

'He's gone,' she said.

'What?'

'He's gone. He's left me.'

'He's done that before. He'll be back.'

'I know, but I'm afraid this time. He didn't go to his office. I hope he's just drunk somewhere and – but this time I'm afraid. Nick, do you think he's really in love with that girl?'

'He seems to think he is.'

'Did he tell you he was?'

'That wouldn't mean anything.'

'Do you think it would do any good to have a talk with her?'

'No.'

'Why don't you? Do you think she's in love with him?'

'No.'

'What's the matter with you?' she asked irritably.

'No. I'm not at home.'

'What? Oh, you mean you're some place where you can't talk?'

'That's it.'

'Are you – are you at her house?'

'Yes.'

'Is she there?'

'No.'

'Do you think she's with him?'

'I don't know. I don't think so.'

'Will you call me when you can talk, or, better still, will you come up to see me?'

'Sure,' I promised, and hung up.

Mimi was looking at me with amusement in her blue eyes. 'Somebody's taking my brat's affairs seriously?' When I did not answer her, she laughed and asked: 'Is Dorry still being the maiden in distress?'

'I suppose so.'

'She will be, too, as long as she can get anybody to believe in it. And you, of all people, to be fooled, you who are afraid to believe that – well – that I, for instance, am ever telling the truth.'

'That's a thought,' I said. The door-bell rang before I could go on.

Mimi let the doctor in – he was a roly-poly elderly man with a stoop and a waddle – and took him into Gilbert.

I opened the table-drawer again and looked at the bonds, Postal Telegraph & Cable 5s, Sao Paulo City 6½s, American Type Founders 6s, Certain-teed Products 5½s, Upper Austria 6½s, United Drugs 5s, Philippine Railway 4s, Tokio Electric Lighting 6s, about sixty thousand dollars at face value, I judged, and – guessing – between a quarter and a third of that at the market.

When the door-bell rang I shut the drawer and let Macaulay in.

He looked tired. He sat down without taking off his overcoat and said: 'Well, tell me the worst. What was he up to here?'

'I don't know yet, except that he gave Mimi some bonds and a cheque.'

'I know that.' He fumbled in his pocket and gave me a letter:

DEAR HERBERT:

I am today giving Mrs Mimi Jorgensen the securities listed below and a ten thousand dollar cheque on the Park Ave Trust dated Jan. 3. Please arrange to have sufficient money there on that date to cover it. I would suggest that you sell some more of the utility bonds, but use your own judgement. I find that I cannot spend any more time in New York at present and probably will not be able to get back here for several months, but will communicate with you from time to time. I am sorry I will not be able to wait over to see you and Charles tonight.

Yours truly,
CLYDE MILLER WYNANT

Under the sprawling signature was a list of the bonds.

'How'd it come to you?' I asked.

'By messenger. What do you suppose he was paying her for?'

I shook my head. 'I tried to find out. She said he was "providing for her and his children".'

'That's likely, as likely as that she'd tell the truth.'

'About these bonds,' I asked, 'I thought you had all his property in your hands?'

'I thought so too, but I didn't have these, didn't know he had them.' He put his elbows on his knees, his head in his hands. 'If all the things I don't know were laid end to end . . .'

XXX

MIMI came in with the doctor, said, 'Oh, how do you do,' a little stiffly to Macaulay, and shook hands with him. 'This is Doctor Grant, Mr Macaulay, Mr Charles.'

'How's the patient?' I asked.

Doctor Grant cleared his throat and said he didn't think there was anything seriously the matter with Gilbert, effects of a beating, slight haemorrhage of course, should rest, though. He cleared his throat again and said he was happy to have met us, and Mimi showed him out.

'What happened to the boy?' Macaulay asked me.

'Wynant sent him on a wild-goose chase over to Julia's apartment and he ran into a tough copper.'

Mimi returned from the door. 'Has Mr Charles told you about the bonds and the cheque?' she asked.

'I had a note from Mr Wynant saying he was giving them to you,' Macaulay said.

'Then there will be no – '

'Difficulty? Not that I know of.'

She relaxed a little and her eyes lost some of their coldness. 'I didn't see why there should be, but he' – pointing at me – 'likes to frighten me.'

Macaulay smiled politely. 'May I ask whether Mr Wynant said anything about his plans?'

'He said something about going away, but I don't suppose I was listening very attentively. I don't remember whether he told me when he was going or where.'

I grunted to show scepticism; Macaulay pretended he believed her. 'Did he say anything that you could repeat to me about Julia Wolf, or about his difficulties, or about anything connected with the murder at all?' he asked.

She shook her head emphatically. 'Not a word I could either repeat or couldn't, not a word at all. I asked him about it, but you know how unsatisfactory he can be when he wants. I couldn't get as much as a grunt out of him about it.'

I asked the question Macaulay seemed too polite to ask: 'What did he talk about?'

'Nothing really, except ourselves and the children, particularly Gil. He was very anxious to see him and waited nearly an hour, hoping he'd come home. He asked about Dorry, but didn't seem very interested.'

'Did he say anything about having written Gilbert?'

'Not a word. I can repeat our whole conversation, if you want me to. I didn't know he was coming, he didn't even phone from downstairs. The door-bell just rang and when I went to the door there he was, looking a lot older than when I'd seen him last and even thinner, and I said: "Why, Clyde" or something like that, and he said: "Are you alone?" I told him I was and he came in. Then he – '

The door-bell rang and she went to answer it.

'What do you think of it?' Macaulay asked in a low voice.

'When I start believing Mimi,' I said, 'I hope I have sense enough not to admit it.'

She returned from the door with Guild and Andy. Guild nodded to me and shook hands with Macaulay, then turned to Mimi and said: 'Well, ma'am, I'll have to ask you to tell – '

Macaulay interrupted him: 'Suppose you let me tell what I have to tell first, Lieutenant. It belongs ahead of Mrs Jorgensen's story and – '

Guild waved a big hand at the lawyer. 'Go ahead.' He sat down on an end of the sofa.

Macaulay told him what he had told me that morning. When he mentioned having told it to me that morning Guild glanced bitterly at me, once, and thereafter ignored me completely. Guild did not interrupt Macaulay, who told his story clearly and concisely. Twice Mimi started to say something, but each time broke off to listen. When Macaulay had finished, he handed Guild the note about the bonds and cheque. 'That came by messenger this afternoon.'

Guild read the note very carefully and addressed Mimi: 'Now then, Mrs Jorgensen.'

She told him what she had told us about Wynant's visit, elaborating the details as he patiently questioned her, but sticking to her story that he had refused to say a word about anything connected with Julia Wolf or her murder, that in giving her the bonds and cheque he had simply said that he wished to provide for her and the children, and that though he had said he was going away she did not know where or when. She seemed not at all disturbed by everybody's obvious disbelief. She wound up smiling, saying: 'He's a sweet man in a lot of ways, but quite mad.'

'You mean he's really insane, do you?' Guild asked; 'not just nutty?'

'Yes.'

'What makes you think that?'

'Oh, you'd have to live with him really to know how mad he is,' she replied airily.

Guild seemed dissatisfied. 'What kind of clothes was he wearing?'

'A brown suit and brown overcoat and hat and I think brown shoes and a white shirt and a greyish necktie with either red or reddish-brown figures in it.'

Guild jerked his head at Andy. 'Tell 'em.'

Andy went out.

Guild scratched his jaw and frowned thoughtfully. The rest of us watched him. When he stopped scratching, he looked at Mimi and Macaulay, but not at me, and asked: 'Any of you know anybody that's got the initials of D. W.Q.?'

Macaulay shook his head from side to side slowly.

Mimi said: 'No. Why?'

Guild looked at me now. 'Well?'

'I don't know them.'

'Why?' Mimi repeated.

Guild said, 'Try to remember back. He'd most likely've had dealings with Wynant.'

'How far back?' Macaulay asked.

'That's hard to say right now. Maybe a few months, maybe a few years. He'd be a pretty large man, big bones, big belly, and maybe lame.'

Macaulay shook his head again. 'I don't remember anybody like that.'

'Neither do I,' Mimi said, 'but I'm bursting with curiosity. I wish you'd tell us what it's all about.'

'Sure, I'll tell you.' Guild took a cigar from his vest pocket, looked at it, returned it to the pocket. 'A dead man like that's buried under the floor of Wynant's shop.'

I said: 'Ah.'

Mimi put both hands to her mouth and said nothing. Her eyes were round and glassy.

Macaulay, frowning, asked: 'Are you sure?'

Guild sighed. 'Now you know that ain't something anybody would guess at,' he said wearily.

Macaulay's face flushed and he smiled sheepishly. 'That was a silly question. How did you happen to find him – it?'

'Well, Mr Charles here kept hinting that we ought to pay more attention to that shop, so, figuring that Mr Charles here is a man that's liable to know a lot more things than he tells anybody right out, I sent some men around this morning to see what they could find. We'd give it the once-over before and hadn't turned up nothing, but this time I told 'em to take the dump apart, because Mr Charles here had said we ought to pay more attention to it. And Mr Charles here was right.' He looked at me with cool un-friendliness. 'By and by they found a corner of the cement floor looking a little newer maybe than the rest and they cracked it and there was the mortal remains of Mr D. W. Q. What do you think of that?'

Macaulay said: 'I think it was a damned good guess of Charles's.' He turned to me. 'How did you –'

Guild interrupted him. 'I don't think you ought to say

that. When you call it just a guess, you ain't giving Mr Charles here the proper credit for being as smart as he is.'

Macaulay was puzzled by Guild's tone. He looked questioningly at me.

'I'm being stood in the corner for not telling Lieutenant Guild about our conversation this morning,' I explained.

'There's that,' Guild agreed calmly, 'among other things.'

Mimi laughed, and smiled apologetically at Guild when he stared at her.

'How was Mr D. W. Q. killed?' I asked.

Guild hesitated, as if making up his mind whether to reply, then moved his big shoulders slightly and said: 'I don't know yet, or how long ago. I haven't seen the remains yet, what there is of them, and the Medical Examiner wasn't through the last I heard.'

'What there is of them?' Macaulay repeated.

'Uh-huh. He'd been sawed up in pieces and buried in lime or something so there wasn't much flesh left on him, according to the report I got, but his clothes had been stuck in with him rolled up in a bundle, and enough was left of the inside ones to tell us something. There was part of a cane, too, with a rubber tip. That's why we thought he might be lame, and we – ' He broke off as Andy came in. 'Well?'

Andy shook his head gloomily. 'Nobody sees him come, nobody sees him go. What was that joke about a guy being so thin he had to stand in the same place twice to throw a shadow?'

I laughed – not at the joke – and said: 'Wynant's not that thin, but he's thin enough, say as thin as the paper in that cheque and in those letters people have been getting.'

'What's that?' Guild demanded, his face reddening, his eyes angry and suspicious.

'He's dead. He's been dead a long time except on paper. I'll give you even money they're his bones in the grave with the fat, lame man's clothes.'

Macaulay leaned towards me. 'Are you sure of that, Charles?'

Guild snarled at me: 'What are you trying to pull?'

'There's the bet if you want it. Who'd go to all that trouble with a corpse and then leave the easiest thing of all to get rid of – the clothes – untouched unless they – '

'But they weren't untouched. They – '

'Of course not. That wouldn't look right. They'd have to be partly destroyed, only enough left to tell you what they were supposed to tell. I bet the initials were plenty conspicuous.'

'I don't know,' Guild said with less heat. 'They were on a belt buckle.'

I laughed.

Mimi said angrily: 'That's ridiculous, Nick. How could that be Clyde? You know he was here this afternoon. You know he – '

'Sh-h-h. It's very silly of you to play along with him,' I told her. 'Wynant's dead, your children are probably his heirs, that's more money than you've got over there in the drawer. What do you want to take part of the loot for when you can get it all?'

'I don't know what you mean,' she said. She was very pale.

Macaulay said: 'Charles thinks Wynant wasn't here this afternoon and that you were given those securities and the cheque by somebody else, or perhaps stole them yourself. Is that it?' he asked me.

'Practically.'

'But that's ridiculous,' she insisted.

'Be sensible, Mimi,' I said. 'Suppose Wynant was killed three months ago and his corpse disguised as somebody else. He's supposed to have gone away leaving powers of attorney with Macaulay. All right, then, the estate's completely in Macaulay's hands for ever and ever, or at least until he finishes plundering it, because you can't even – '

Macaulay stood up saying: 'I don't know what you're getting at, Charles, but I'm – '

'Take it easy,' Guild told him. 'Let him have his say out.'

'He killed Wynant and he killed Julia and he killed Nunheim,' I assured Mimi. 'What do you want to do? Be next on the list? You ought to know damned well that once you've come to his aid by saying you've seen Wynant alive – because that's his weak spot, being the only person up to now who claims to have seen Wynant since October – he's not going to take any chances on having you change your mind – not when it's only a matter of knocking you off with the same gun and putting the blame on Wynant. And what are you doing it for? For those few crummy bonds in the drawer, a fraction of what you get your hands on through your children if we prove Wynant's dead.'

Mimi turned to Macaulay and said: 'You rat!'

Guild gaped at her, more surprised by that than by anything else that had been said.

Macaulay started to move. I did not wait to see what he meant to do, but slammed his chin with my left fist. The punch was all right, it landed solidly and dropped him, but I felt a burning sensation on my left side and knew I had torn the bullet-wound open.

'What do you want me to do?' I growled at Guild. 'Put him in cellophane for you?'

XXXI

It was nearly three in the morning when I let myself into our apartment at the Normandie. Nora, Dorothy, and Larry Crowley were in the living-room, Nora and Larry playing backgammon, Dorothy reading a newspaper.

'Did Macaulay really kill them?' Nora asked immediately.

'Yes. Did the morning papers have anything about Wynant?'

Dorothy said: 'No, just about Macaulay being arrested. Why?'

'Macaulay killed him too.'

Nora said: 'Really?' Larry said: 'I'll be damned.' Dorothy began to cry. Nora looked at Dorothy in surprise. Dorothy sobbed: 'I want to go home to Mamma.'

Larry said not very eagerly: 'I'll be glad to take you home if . . .'

Dorothy said she wanted to go. Nora fussed over her but did not try to talk her out of going. Larry, trying not to look too unwilling, found his hat and coat. He and Dorothy left.

Nora shut the door behind them and leaned against it. 'Explain that to me, Mr Charalambides,' she said.

I shook my head.

She sat on the sofa beside me. 'Now out with it. If you skip a single word, I'll – '

'I'd have to have a drink before I could do any talking.'

She cursed me and brought me a drink. 'Has he confessed?'

'Why should he? You can't plead guilty of murder in the first degree. There were too many murders – and at least two of them were too obviously done in cold blood – for the District Attorney to let him plead guilty of second-degree murder. There's nothing for him to do but fight it out.'

'But he did commit them?'

'Sure.'

She pushed my glass down from my mouth. 'Stop stalling and tell me about it.'

'Well, it figures out that he and Julia had been gypping Wynant for some time. He'd dropped a lot of money in the market and he'd found out about her past – as Morelli hinted – and the pair of them teamed up on the old man. We're sticking accountants on Macaulay's books and Wynant's and shouldn't have much trouble tracing some of the loot from one to the other.'

'Then you don't know positively that he was robbing Wynant?'

'Sure we know. It doesn't click any other way. The chances are Wynant was going away on a trip the 3rd of October, because he did draw five thousand dollars out of the bank in cash, but didn't close up his shop and give up his apartment. That was done by Macaulay a few days later. Wynant was killed at Macaulay's in Scarsdale on the night of the 3rd. We know that because on the morning of the 4th, when Macaulay's cook, who slept at home, came to work, Macaulay met her at the door with some kind of trumped-up complaint and two weeks' wages and fired her on the spot, not letting her in the house to find any corpses or blood-stains.'

'How did you find that out? Don't skip details.'

'Ordinary routine. Naturally after we grabbed him we went to his office and house to see what we could find out – you know, where-were-you-on-the-night-of-June-6, 1894-stuff – and the present cook said she'd only been working for him since the 8th of October, and that led to that. We also found a table with a very faint trace of what we hope is human blood not quite scrubbed out. The scientific boys are making shavings of it now to see if they can soak out any results for us.' (It turned out to be beef-blood.)

'Then you're not sure he – '

'Stop saying that. Of course we're sure. That's the only way it clicks. Wynant had found out that Julia and Macaulay were gypping him and also thought, rightly or wrongly, that Julia and Macaulay were cheating on him – and we know he was jealous – so he went up there to confront him with whatever proof he had, and Macaulay, with prison looking him in the face, killed the old man. Now don't say we're not sure. It doesn't make any sense otherwise. Well, there he is with a corpse, one of the harder things to get rid of. Can I stop to take a swallow of whisky?'

'Just one,' Nora said. 'But this is just a theory, isn't it?'

'Call it any name you like. It's good enough for me.'

'But I thought everybody was supposed to be considered innocent until they were proved guilty and if there was any reasonable doubt, they – '

'That's for juries, not detectives. You find the guy you think did the murder and you slam him in the can and let everybody know you think he's guilty and put his picture all over the newspapers, and the District Attorney builds up the best theory he can on what information you've got and meanwhile you pick up additional details here and there and people who recognize his picture in the paper – as well as people who'd think he was innocent if you hadn't arrested him – come in and tell you things about him and presently you've got him sitting on the electric chair.' (Two days later a woman in Brooklyn identified Macaulay as a George Foley who for the past three months had been renting an apartment from her.)

'But that seems so loose.'

'When murders are committed by mathematics,' I said, 'you can solve them by mathematics. Most of them aren't and this one wasn't. I don't want to go against your idea of what's right and wrong, but when I say he probably dissected the body so he could carry it into town in bags I'm only saying what seems most probable. That would be on the 6th of October or later, because it wasn't until then that he laid off the two mechanics Wynant had working in the shop – Prentice and McNaughton – and shut it up. So he buried Wynant under the floor, buried him with a fat man's clothes and a lame man's stick and a belt marked D. W. Q., all arranged so they wouldn't get too much of the lime – or whatever he used to eat off the dead man's features and flesh – on them, and he re-cemented the floor over the grave. Between police routine and publicity we've got more than a fair chance of finding out where he bought or otherwise got the clothes and stick and the cement.' (We traced the cement to him later – he had bought it from a coal and wood dealer uptown – but had no luck with the other things.)

'I hope so,' she said, not too hopefully.

'So now that's taken care of. By renewing the lease on the shop and keeping it vacant – supposedly waiting for Wynant to return – he can make sure – reasonably sure – that nobody will discover the grave, and if it is accidentally discovered, then fat Mr D. W. Q. – by that time Wynant's bones would be pretty bare and you can't tell whether a man was thin or fat by his skeleton – was murdered by Wynant, which explains why Wynant has made himself scarce. That taken care of, Macaulay forges the power of attorney and, with Julia's help, settles down to the business of gradually transferring the late Clyde's money to themselves. Now I'm going theoretical again. Julia doesn't like murder, and she's frightened, and he's not too sure she won't weaken on him. That's why he makes her break with Morelli – giving Wynant's jealousy as an excuse. He's afraid she might confide to Morelli in a weak moment and, as the time draws near for her still closer friend, Face Peppler, to get out of prison, he gets more and more worried. He's been safe there as long as Face stayed in, because she's not likely to put anything dangerous in a letter that has to pass through the warden's hands, but now ... Well, he starts to plan, and then all hell breaks loose. Mimi and her children arrive and start hunting for Wynant and I come to town and am in touch with them and he thinks I'm helping them. He decides to play safe on Julia by putting her out of the way. Like it so far?'

'Yes, but ...'

'It gets worse as it goes along,' I assured her. 'On his way here for lunch that day he stops and phones his office, pretending he's Wynant, and making that appointment at the Plaza, the idea being to establish Wynant's presence in town. When he leaves here he goes to the Plaza and asks people if they've seen Wynant, to make that plausible, and for the same reason phones his office to ask if any further word has come in from Wynant, and phones Julia. She tells him she's expecting Mimi and she tells him Mimi thought she was lying when she said she didn't know where Wynant was, and Julia probably sounds pretty frightened. So he decides he's got to beat Mimi to the interview and he does. He beats it over there and kills her. He's a terrible shot. I saw him shoot during the war. It's likely he missed her with the first shot, the one that hit the telephone, and didn't succeed in killing her right away with the other four, but he probably thought she was dead, and, anyhow, he had to get out before Mimi arrived, so he dropped the piece of Wynant's chain that he had brought along as a clincher – and his having saved that for three months makes it look as if he'd intended killing her from the beginning – and scoots over to the engineer Hermann's office, where he takes advantage of the breaks and fixes himself up with an alibi. The two things he doesn't expect – couldn't very well have foreseen – are that Nunheim, hanging around trying to get at the girl, had seen him leave her apartment – may even have heard the shot – and that Mimi, with blackmail in her heart, was going to conceal the chain for use in shaking down her ex-husband. That's why he had to go down to Philadelphia and send me that wire and the letter to himself and one to Aunt Alice later – if Mimi thinks Wynant's throwing suspicion on her she'll get mad enough to give the police the evidence she's got against him. Her desire to hurt Jorgensen nearly gummed that up, though. Macaulay, by the way, knew Jorgensen was Rosewater. Right after he killed Wynant he had detectives look Mimi and her family up in Europe – their interest in the estate made them potentially dangerous – and the detectives found out who Jorgensen was. We found the reports in Macaulay's files. He pretended he was getting the information for Wynant, of course. Then he started worrying about me, about my not thinking Wynant guilty and – '

'And why didn't you?'

'Why should he write letters antagonizing Mimi, the one who was helping him by holding back incriminating evidence? That's why I thought the chain had been planted

186

when she did turn it in, only I was a little bit too willing to believe she had done the planting. Morelli worried Macaulay, too, because he didn't want suspicion thrown on anybody who might, in clearing themselves, throw it in the wrong direction. Mimi was all right, because she'd throw it back on Wynant, but everybody else was out. Suspicion thrown on Wynant was the one thing that was guaranteed to keep anybody from suspecting that Wynant was dead, and if Macaulay hadn't killed Wynant, then there was no reason for his having killed either of the others. The most obvious thing in the whole lay-out and the key to the whole lay-out was that Wynant had to be dead.'

'You mean you thought that from the beginning?' Nora demanded, fixing me with a stern eye.

'No, darling, though I ought to be ashamed of myself for not seeing it, but once I heard there was a corpse under the floor, I wouldn't have cared if doctors swore it was a woman's I'd have insisted it was Wynant's. It had to be. It was the one right thing.'

'I guess you're awfully tired. That must be what makes you talk like this.'

'Then he had Nunheim to worry about too. After pointing the finger at Morelli, just to show the police he was being useful, he went to see Macaulay. I'm guessing again, sweetheart. I had a phone-call from a man who called himself Albert Norman, and the conversation ended with a noise on his end of the wire. My guess is that Nunheim went to see Macaulay and demanded some dough to keep quiet and, when Macaulay tried to bluff him, Nunheim said he'd show him and called me up to make a date with me to see if I'd buy his information – and Macaulay grabbed the phone and gave Nunheim something, if only a promise, but when Guild and I had our little talk with Nunheim, and he ran out on us, then he phoned Macaulay and demanded real action, probably a lump sum, with a promise to beat it out of town, away from us meddling sleuths. We do know he called up that afternoon – Macaulay's telephone-operator remembers a Mr Albert Norman calling up, and she remembers that Macaulay went out right after talking to him, so don't get snooty about this – uh – reconstruction of mine. Macaulay wasn't silly enough to think Nunheim was to be trusted even if he paid him, so he lured him down to this spot he had probably picked out ahead of time and let him have it – and that took care of that.'

'Probably,' Nora said.

'It's a word you've got to use a lot in this business. The letter to Gilbert was only for the purpose of showing that Wynant had a key to the girl's apartment, and sending Gilbert there was only a way of making sure that he'd fall into the hands of the police, who'd squeeze him and not let him keep the information about the letter and the key to himself. Then Mimi finally comes through with the watch-chain, but meanwhile another worry comes up. She's persuaded Guild to suspect me a little. I've an idea that when Macaulay came to me this morning with that hooey he intended to get me up to Scarsdale and knock me off, making me number three on the list of Wynant's victims. Maybe he just changed his mind, maybe he thought I was suspicious, too willing to go up there without policemen. Anyhow, Gilbert's lie about having seen Wynant gave him another idea. If he could get somebody to say they had seen Wynant and stick to it . . . Now this part we know definitely.'

'Thank God.'

'He went to see Mimi this afternoon – riding up two floors above hers and walking down so the elevator boys wouldn't remember having carried him to her door – and made her a proposition. He told her there was no question about Wynant's guilt, but that it was doubtful if the police would ever catch him. Meanwhile he, Macaulay, had the whole estate in his hands. He couldn't take a chance on appropriating any of it, but he'd fix it so she could – if she would split with him. He'd give her these bonds he had in his pocket and this cheque, but she'd have to say that Wynant had given them to her and she'd have to send this note, which he also had, over to Macaulay as if from Wynant. He assured her that Wynant, a fugitive, could not show up to deny his gift, and, except for herself and her children, there was no one else who had any interest in the estate, any reason for questioning the deal. Mimi's not very sensible where she sees a chance to make a profit, so it was all O.K. with her, and he had what he wanted – somebody who'd seen Wynant alive. He warned her that everybody would think Wynant was paying her for some service, but if she simply denied it there would be nothing anybody could prove.'

'Then what he told you this morning about Wynant instructing him to give her any amount she asked for was simply in preparation?'

'Maybe; maybe it was an earlier fumbling towards that idea. Now are you satisfied with what we've got on him?'

'Yes, in a way. There seems to be enough of it, but it's not very neat.'

'It's neat enough to send him to the chair,' I said, 'and that's all that counts. It takes care of all the angles and I can't think of any other theory that would. Naturally it wouldn't hurt to find the pistol, and the typewriter he used for the Wynant letters, and they must be somewhere around where he can get at them when he needs them.' (We found them in the Brooklyn apartment he had rented as George Foley.)

'Have it your own way,' she said, 'but I always thought detectives waited until they had every little detail fixed in – '

'And then wonder why the suspects had time to get to the farthest country that has no extradition treaty.'

She laughed. 'All right, all right. Still want to leave for San Francisco tomorrow?'

'Not unless you're in a hurry. Let's stick around a while. This excitement has put us behind in our drink.'

'It's all right by me. What do you think will happen to Mimi and Dorothy and Gilbert now?'

'Nothing new. They'll go on being Mimi and Dorothy and Gilbert just as you and I will go on being us and the Quinns will go on being the Quinns. Murder doesn't round out anybody's life except the murdered's and sometimes the murderer's.'

'That may be,' Nora said, 'but it's all pretty unsatisfactory.'

READ MORE IN PENGUIN

In every corner of the world, on every subject under the sun, Penguin represents quality and variety – the very best in publishing today.

For complete information about books available from Penguin – including Puffins, Penguin Classics and Arkana – and how to order them, write to us at the appropriate address below. Please note that for copyright reasons the selection of books varies from country to country.

In the United Kingdom: Please write to *Dept. EP, Penguin Books Ltd, Bath Road, Harmondsworth, West Drayton, Middlesex UB7 0DA*

In the United States: Please write to *Consumer Sales, Penguin Putnam Inc., P.O. Box 999, Dept. 17109, Bergenfield, New Jersey 07621-0120.* VISA and MasterCard holders call 1-800-253-6476 to order Penguin titles

In Canada: Please write to *Penguin Books Canada Ltd, 10 Alcorn Avenue, Suite 300, Toronto, Ontario M4V 3B2*

In Australia: Please write to *Penguin Books Australia Ltd, P.O. Box 257, Ringwood, Victoria 3134*

In New Zealand: Please write to *Penguin Books (NZ) Ltd, Private Bag 102902, North Shore Mail Centre, Auckland 10*

In India: Please write to *Penguin Books India Pvt Ltd, 210 Chiranjiv Tower, 43 Nehru Place, New Delhi 110 019*

In the Netherlands: Please write to *Penguin Books Netherlands bv, Postbus 3507, NL-1001 AH Amsterdam*

In Germany: Please write to *Penguin Books Deutschland GmbH, Metzlerstrasse 26, 60594 Frankfurt am Main*

In Spain: Please write to *Penguin Books S. A., Bravo Murillo 19, 1° B, 28015 Madrid*

In Italy: Please write to *Penguin Italia s.r.l., Via Benedetto Croce 2, 20094 Corsico, Milano*

In France: Please write to *Penguin France, Le Carré Wilson, 62 rue Benjamin Baillaud, 31500 Toulouse*

In Japan: Please write to *Penguin Books Japan Ltd, Kaneko Building, 2-3-25 Koraku, Bunkyo-Ku, Tokyo 112*

In South Africa: Please write to *Penguin Books South Africa (Pty) Ltd, Private Bag X14, Parkview, 2122 Johannesburg*

READ MORE IN PENGUIN

A SELECTION OF CRIME AND MYSTERY

The Blunderer Patricia Highsmith

Walter Stackhouse wishes his wife was dead. His wish comes true when Clara's body is found at the bottom of a cliff. But there are uncanny similarities between her death and that of a woman called Helen Kimmel – murdered by her husband... 'Almost unputdownable' – *Observer*

Death of a Partner Janet Neel

His relationship with wilful girlfriend Francesca on the rocks, a harassed Detective Chief Inspector John McLeish is assigned to the case of missing Angela Morgan. An attractive, wealthy lobbyist, and fiancée to a high-ranking government minister, Angela courted success – and the envy of her detractors. When her badly decomposed body is found a week later, the shock waves ripple through Whitehall, and only the murderer knows why.

Maigret and the Madwoman Georges Simenon

Maigret's underlings called her the Madwoman. Yet in fact she was a respectable widow who was convinced that someone followed her when she spent the afternoons in the park. The old lady claimed that it was a matter of life and death; she demanded an interview with her hero, Chief Superintendent Maigret. He agreed. But before he can do so, she is murdered.

The Thirty-Nine Steps John Buchan

In this gripping tale of the hunt for a wanted man – the innocent Richard Hannay – John Buchan created one of the most famous and admired thrillers of all time. With the creation of Richard Hannay, a South African mining engineer and war hero, John Buchan established himself as one of Britain's finest writers of suspense stories.

Vanishing Ladies Ed McBain

A peaceful lake, a cabin in the country, and each other... It looked as though it was going to be an idyllic holiday for Phil Colby and his fiancée Anne. But then Anne disappears from her motel room, and Phil finds a red-haired hooker in her place...